LAST TIDE

PRAISE FOR *LAST TIDE*

"Set in a sinister world of corporate blurrers and digital scrubbers, this profound and powerful novel sneaks up on the reader, ebbing and flowing so quietly that no one within its reach is fully prepared for the deadly sharpness of real life." —Rosie Chard, author of *The Eavesdroppers* and *The Insistent Garden*

"*Last Tide* takes us on a fully satisfying, dystopic adventure with a motley crew of islanders. Unpredictable nature and expansionist industries compete in edgy plot lines that come together with Zuliani's highly skilled cross weave of imagery, allegory, and philosophical thought. This novel is like the futuristic fashion designed by its entrepreneurial villain: it feels alive, current, even as it anticipates the next catastrophic wave." —Thea Bowering, author of *Love at Last Sight*

"Andy Zuliani's writing is hyper-alive to landscape and culture of the West Coast. Dense, rich, evocative prose and imagery pull us into the narrative like an undertow. His debut novel submerges and tumbles us in a powerful wave of beauty and warning." —Karen Hofmann, author of *A Brief View from the Coastal Suite* and *Echolocation*

"There is a telling phrase early in Andy Zuliani's remarkable debut, *Last Tide*: 'once the process gets going, it's hard to stop.' The multiple, layered, and entangled processes at the heart of this mesmerising story—personal grief and trauma, surveillance and data collection, real estate development and the looming presence of inevitable natural disaster—unfold, as the narrative does, with the precision of intricate clock-work. Like a calm coastal harbour, beneath the still surface of Zuliani's prose the human heart thrums against the pressures formed by the collision of capital and geology. This is the writing we need—compassionate, clear eyed, undaunted—in an age gripped by apocalyptic fear." —Stephen Collis, author of *A History of the Theories of Rain*

LAST

ANDY
ZULIANI

TIDE

NEWEST PRESS
EDMONTON, AB

Library and Archives Canada Cataloguing in Publication

Title: Last tide / Andy Zuliani.
Names: Zuliani, Andy, author.
Series: Nunatak first fiction series ; no. 56.
Description: Series statement: Nunatak first fiction series ; 56
Identifiers: Canadiana (print) 20200405543 | Canadiana (ebook) 20200405551 |
ISBN 9781774390344 (softcover) |
ISBN 9781774390351 (EPUB)
Classification: LCC PS8649.U45 L37 2021 | DDC C813/.6—dc23

NeWest Press wishes to acknowledge that the land on which we operate is Treaty 6 territory and a traditional meeting ground and home for many Indigenous Peoples, including Cree, Saulteaux, Niitsitapi (Blackfoot), Métis, and Nakota Sioux.

Board Editor: Doug Barbour
Cover design & typesetting: Kate Hargreaves
(texture creative commons by Ketan Saptasagare via Unsplash)
Author photograph: Jamie Staples
All Rights Reserved

NeWest Press acknowledges the Canada Council for the Arts, the Alberta Foundation for the Arts, and the Edmonton Arts Council for support of our publishing program. This project is funded in part by the Government of Canada.

201, 8540 – 109 Street
Edmonton, AB T6G 1E6
780.432.9427
NeWest Press   www.newestpress.com

No bison were harmed in the making of this book.
PRINTED AND BOUND IN CANADA
1 2 3 4 5 23 22 21

for Daryn

PART ONE: REFORMATTING

CHAPTER ONE

S HE DOESN'T BLUR THEM, THAT'S WIN'S JOB, BUT she does feel that swipe, top to bottom, when she sees their faces. As if the process has already started in her head. She doesn't even actuate the shutter; that all happens on its own. It's her job to advance, between clicks, and provide material. So if she does see the faces blur, maybe around hour six or seven when the repetition starts to get to her, she thinks of Win, her quick swipe on the trackpad, the pixelating smudge. Finishing her work. She's viewed the results so many times that, driving in the van, she sees the faces all pre-blurred, looking at the camera, looking at her, and she doesn't know whether to wave or hide her face.

But it's a surprise how few people she sees, even after work on a weekday, even on weekends. She comes to realize that streets aren't really about locomotion, but division of plots and zones. It's different on foot, with the presence of decision, of contingency: a street walked on is a street made real. When she's in the van, she's not there. Ana will now and then catch figures coming out of doorways, bodies standing at bus stops or in line, always bent towards her, looking. Few of the frozen get caught off guard, and Win deals with the faces they angle over shoulders and out of windows, wipes them clean of curiosity and confusion. The clicks are triggered by time, not distance. Pedestrians are photographed as they walk alongside her, as, knowingly or not, they are captured over and over again. Win tells her that, when this happens, the sidewalk looks like a parade of clones on their way to the factory. She scrolls through the line, and clears their identical faces one by one.

The grid is simple. She extends down a road, reaches the end, turns the corner, and retracts. The handbook says that it is easier to think of yourself in this way—from a fixed, satellite's-eye view—instead of at ground level, even though the latter is the vantage point of their products. The handbook is right, especially when the lay of the streets shifts or pivots around some central point and disorientation is a real risk. Maintaining this top-down view is harder in old cities, with their streets radiating like spokes from a hub, spliced by canals, viaducts, and ad hoc passages just wide enough for the van to fit through. But she has little trouble keeping today's fixed grid of industrial lots from rotating in her mind. She does not think of straight, or left, or even north- or south-west, but instead only the twin coordinates of x and y. If this seems difficult to conceptualize, it doesn't stay that way.

The handbook is wrong about a few things. It says that pedestrians might try to stop you; they might stand in front of the van and pose for a picture. This hasn't happened to her or any of the other drivers she knows. A coworker says she had a woman lift up her blouse and flash the camera. She asked Win, who said that if that did happen, she would just blur it out. She doesn't really believe the other driver's story, though. She knows the truth: that he is, she is, invisible. She's been driving for three years and not once has a passerby mugged for her camera, posed, or even waved. The consensus seems to be that they don't exist. The van is large, and the camera rigging is hardly discreet, but pedestrians look at them quickly and then avert their eyes. The man who trained her joked that they were afraid she'd steal their soul, and that she shouldn't take it personally. She doesn't. She hears the camera click faintly behind her head, and in her mind she wipes their faces clean.

The guide also says it's a good way to get to know a city, driving the van, but Ana had lived here for twenty years before the contract. She doesn't feel a sense of discovery, then, but instead one of reformatting. Streets she knew from her late twenties are repaved by the camera, cleaned of their memories, rendered into the official, sellable view. Clear, demarcated, and without emotional charge. Last week she drove the van like a pressure washer along the driveway's edge of her childhood home. She looked, from the van, into her old bedroom. Only then did she slow down, the camera clicking out the time, the flash bouncing in sheets off of the darkened window. The images were fed in that evening, the scene scrubbed and encoded. The strangers' car in the open garage had its licence plate blurred—Win's handiwork. But Ana's left her face, just a beige wrinkle in the bedroom window, intact.

Licence plates are blurred. Faces are blurred. Bus stop ads stay, though, depending on the city and its laws, their phone numbers may be blurred. The faces on the ads remain. House numbers are left intact, but names on mailboxes are blurred. Billboards stay, netting their advertisers a windfall of advertisement. Profanity painted on anything—walls, billboards, bus benches, pavement, shop windows—is usually left untouched, though this is up to the blurrer's discretion. Win leaves all but the worst, and those she prints out before blurring. Some employees choose to go through the day's images and blur out faces first, and then words and numbers; some do both at once. Win tells Ana that infant's faces come pre-blurred, and that young children are often moving too erratically for the camera's exposure to catch in any violating detail, especially in the late afternoon hours, when the shutter dilates for lost light. The rights of children are a particular concern; their company wants to avoid lawsuit, implication, expense.

Not all of them started as drivers. A handful drove other things—milk trucks, taxicabs, school busses— before switching to delivering images. But these are few. Most drivers are internal hires. Most of these end up in the van on the way down from a higher position. There isn't a euphemism in place for this, it just happens, un-memoed. Ana was in the van from the first day, though she's used to driving for money. This makes her unusual, but it's hard to say how much of this is the circumstances of her hiring, and how much is some kind of in-group favouritism on the part of the lifers, the internals. According to the social strata, those coming down from office jobs, and the few who were around before the project even started, resist the idea that they're working the same position as a subway operator.

Those who are behind the wheel of the van for eight hours a day have a good amount of time to think, especially on the more minimal sections. A highway shift offers the same kind of introspection as a long road trip alone, especially since, unlike the road trip, you're not distracted by thoughts of a final destination. One of the other drivers learned French while the camera clicked out fields of soybean plants for hours along 91 North. Another, an ex-millwright, buys books on tape, leaving them in the vans for the other drivers when he's done with them. But she prefers the more involved driving. She's bored of straight lines. She angles for shifts in knotty downtown cores, where it takes real work to stay oriented and keep from wasting shots backtracking. Whenever possible she takes travel jobs to other cities that she does not know and, over the week, covers their blank streets and alleys until she, and the camera, have seen every boulevard and storefront.

The drivers are encouraged to leave the camera going for the drive back to the depots—the documentation of the fringes and hinterlands in which the vans sleep is of special interest to their clients. Images of near-vacant industrial lots, rezoneable and ripe, are the grist of the real estate mill. This is the new frontier: doubling back. The cities are running out of unused space, and so the cities need to be reformatted. And reformatting is their business.

Ana used to work in the public sphere in a less conflicted sense. When she dropped out of school she wanted a job she could detach herself from, so, despite her comp-sci training, she took a position at BTA. Seeing her former classmates board the trains, briefcases in hand, heading to tech firms and start-ups and security agencies, didn't bother her. There was a certain satisfaction to the work. When she re-examines what she did, the overlap is obvious—she supposes she is, has always been, a person in motion. But in her past life, this tendency was simplified to the point of meditation. Between stations the tunnel was a dark chute, the lights illuminating only a brief figure eight of trackbed, and the rushing of the air around the front car's blunt nose was an even, mantric hum. The controls at hand were minimal, practically binary: forward lever, brake lever, emergency brake, door control. An oval capsule on a stalk gave the speed in red LED, and below it, a matching clock. The difficulty and skill were in the precise use of these few instruments, in staying on exact schedule, in knowing by feel the distance needed to slow the train to a stop without overshooting the platform, even by a few feet. It wasn't as hard for the BTA operators as it was in cities with overlapping tracks, where an unnoticed error in selection would lead, minutes later, to the head-on collision at full speed of two trains full of passengers—but it was not as simple a job as her mother insisted. It was just simple enough for her at that time. She wanted a break to think, a steady, undemanding job. But that was years ago, when she was comfortable in her mind. Now, she looks for distraction, tries to lose herself in the maze.

ON DAYS THAT SHE'S SUCCESSFUL, SHE'S ONLY EVER half in her own head. The satellite view can be taxing, especially towards end of shift, in the seventh hour, when you've rotated your way through mazes since the morning. The older section of the handbook encourages you to think of yourself as a miniature van, seen from above, moving around the map, but she imagines herself as less than this—as an icon, a cursor. In her mind, she is a triangular pointer. Edges blur by five o'clock, and, with the light dying, she heads back. She pulls in, camera still clicking away, and parks the van in its slot in the depot. Only now does the shutter stop. It's hard to shut the cursor off as she makes her way home on the slow, convoluted set of bus rides she's learned; after three years in the van, her brain is programmed to equate movement with mapping. Win says she can see it on her face on the days she gives her a ride home.

This week has Ana recovering old ground, starting with the highway that cuts through the southern end of town and divides it between residential and commercial, then continuing to the commercial zone itself. A real audiobook job, but there aren't any in the van. She drove this section last year, but, with the rapid development of the area—once reserved for the factories that now, in the absence of demand for their products, are unpeopled shells—the images need updating. Post-industrial becoming pre-residential, and at the cutting edge of this transformation, her, camera clicking, driving in silence for eight hours a day in a barren grid of warehouses where condos and offices have begun to bloom.

It is now the fourth day of scanning. The boredom of identical lots, mechanical grey paint spray-gunned across concrete. Each factory, plant, shipping centre an anonymous squatting cube. The sound of the radio at these outer limits of the metropolis fuzzing between stations. Or is it the cement, the rebar, the sleeping asbestos—all this dead matter that insulates these blocks from the signal? Not insulated enough: on her right is a set of lofts, inset into the face of a warehouse, floor-to-ceiling windows lighting up empty living rooms. Next door, an abandoned wholesale furniture depot, guarding itself with cyclone fence, waiting its turn. She takes its picture, or the van does, the image cued and compiled for future use. The rest of the long industrial block is more cyclone fences, more empty warehouses, more plywood windows. She records it all. As she reaches the end of the block, the radio scratches into life: a commercial for an oscillating clothes dryer. The end of the street describes a T with narrow aerials that cut on each side between the last row of buildings and an adjacent lumberyard. Through a gap between structures loom colossal pyramids of wet sawdust. She turns a right that is actually a left, from the top-down view, and, with mute thirty-foot exterior walls rising on each side, the radio falls quiet.

When she emerges, nothing is different, and for a moment she loses the grid. Cells upon cells of identical warehouses, signs weathered smooth, vinyl lettering sun-peeled into strips. The factories in their dilapidation looking like old, battered houses, the new residential units in their brutal geometry and exposed structures looking like factories. Only the alternation between these two giving some sense of trajectory and time, but not direction. She knows that must be going straight, or, north, y, but the referents are gone. The camera clicks out a dozen images of the same, panoramic view: a shallow parking lot, its fence yellowed with rust—a shuttered brickworks—a sidewalk ending abruptly in yellow turf—the cracked asphalt of the road, its black tracery of patchwork—the opposite sidewalk—an empty security kiosk, its automated gate stuck open—pallets stacked in a vacant parking space—around the curve of the camera's orb—now, the same road, from behind, light grey and tire-smoothed, the shining black filler like a kind of writing—behind, in mid-distance, the towering mountains of sawdust, filling the frame—the curb, fractured from the passage of heavy sixteen-wheelers—a many-tiered sign, all its acetate inserts taken out and reinserted upside down—the start of the brief sidewalk—the narrow lot with its rusted fence—the brickworks again, at the end of the loop, its manila siding streaked green from plant matter. The camera clicks one last time as she put the van back into drive.

This is the second-last interior row in a grid of two dozen. At every division of lots, she and the camera look to the side, crosswise, through the set of nested, identical intersections. With each added row, the mirror-within-a-mirror effect grows frame by frame to a narrowing point, the blocks' facing edges enclosing each other like parentheses wrapping around parentheses. The manual names this doubling *positive redundancy*, as the shift in perspective allows them a second, third, fourth chance at capturing information previously obscured by trees, pedestrians, street traffic. But there is little here to interfere: she is the only soul, the only vehicle, the only movement in this grid, and every repeated shot of the same empty street corner reveals the same contentless information, unobscured but for the obscurity of its own repetition. She reaches the end of the row—she thinks—and cuts once again through a narrow lane. One more line of the grid, then, the periphery of the grid itself, then, back to the depot, home.

Her radio cuts out again, and this time she turns the knob to mute. She catches her face's reflection in the screen of the dash-mounted display, which, as always, she has left off. Her phone, its GPS safety net, is buttoned into her jacket pocket. Paper maps on the passenger seat, even these folded, though she'll allow herself them in an emergency. In three years she's learned, as all drivers do, that this job is as complicated as you let it be, but, unlike her coworkers, she has taken this in the opposite direction. She volunteers for the mess, breeds complication willingly. Yet no inner-city runs on the books this week, just this industrial drudge, a challenge in its own right. This work predates the technology that makes it brainless, even if she doesn't; there are entire sections of the manual on cartography, way-finding, chapters she's read over and over, relishing the intricacy of technique, the antiquated, pre-digital tactics of location. They have been scanning the city long before doing so became a hobby. Longer still before this information was freely broadcast under the auspices of public use.

The mountain of sawdust is gone, blocked from view by the monolithic lumber processing plant, the machinery of which these pyramids are the exhaust. Silent, though whether this is temporary or permanent disuse she cannot tell. Win calls Ana and her colleagues vultures, and she's not wrong—here she is, circling these industrial skeletons. As she pulls past there is a deafening, metallic screech, and the saws start up again. Not yet, she thinks. And: If I'm a vulture, what is Win? What follows after carrion, finishes what's left? The backs of these megaplexes, their vulnerable array of loading docks and fire exits, are nothing like their bland, faceless fronts. A colossal dumpster, half off of its concrete pad, passes by, and out of the corner of her eye she sees something small and dark dart up the side and through a crack in the lid. A vision from a past life: rats, startled into motion by the electric hum of the rail and the clatter of steel on steel, disappearing into shadows.

She pushes it back like a physical thing, and focuses on the final row of units, mostly foreclosed warehouses, brick and cinder block under white paint. Mentally she punches twelve-foot windows out of their blank facades, extrudes tennis-court-sized balconies, adds exterior detailing, carves out new facades, doing the work of future architects in her head. And her prediction is correct: a lone green sign marks the whole section for rezoning and redevelopment. It's hard to keep the correct pace, when there's so little to see. She keeps wanting to accelerate, but to speed up above the determined limit means missing key wedges of image. The manual advises drivers to imagine that they are controlling a film projector, to think of the street outside of their windows as a long spool of celluloid that they need to play at the correct rate to maintain the realism of the picture. The *verisimilitude*, a beautiful world. She watches the needle, trying to keep it right at the notch that reads twenty, another thing that she is good at. It doesn't matter how she slows or stops the van—any freeze-frames are removed in the first pass of editing—but she does so with a single, gradual motion, smooth enough that a standing passenger with only one hand on the pole wouldn't even have to shift their weight. A skill she has made obsolete for herself.

Many other transit systems had been phasing out manually-driven subway trains for automated ones, but the cost kept the tax-starved city hesitant and herself employed, for the time being. She returns to this often: what if they had made the switch? Would she then be spared this psychic reformatting, this need for constant distraction, variation? Would she still be a vulture? She slows the van to a rolling stop, grateful for the change, and turns around to head back, halfway down the row, to the exit. Another empty security kiosk, but this gate is automated; it rises for her and she passes through. She checks her watch: she is on schedule for the last item on the list, a roundabout sweep of the outside of the subdivision to explore possibilities of expansion. Standard practice, especially for these kinds of property—once the process gets going, it's hard to stop, and within years entire sub-cities spring up in the vacuum of industrial deserts. And a desert this is: outside the exterior walls of the outermost buildings there is nothing, just sheets of asphalt cut into grids by temporary fencing. Hundreds of yards beyond the final fence, some vacant farmland offers even less resistance. All gone soon, she knows.

And all straight lines. Now that she is outside of it, the industrial zone seems even more sprawling and immense. She accelerates to the designated speed but seems to make no progress against the blank, anonymous walls or the empty lots opposite. It is as if here, in the open, is farther from culture, the human signal. Her mind, yielding, starts to disengage, and whatever few distinguishing details go soft. She nearly coasts right through the red light, and, though the intersection is empty, she hits the brakes hard and waits for the change. The light goes green and she turns left to follow along the zone's eastern edge. She rounds the corner, and, suddenly, it is night: the factories' bulk, their heat-proof and cold-proof walls, blocks out the last of the sun's arc and throws her into blue-black shade. Automatic street lights click on, the halogen bulbs warming up against the early spring air in sporadic flashes. Their flicker against the van's windows, her eye on the speedometer, the late-shift weariness, transports her to precisely where she doesn't want to go, brings her in an irreversible sliding to the same, repeating scene. Nothing worked. Therapy didn't work; a hundred boring conversations with friends and family didn't work. Changing jobs didn't work. The thing waited for her, waited for an opening, whether in dreams or in waking life, and she couldn't close off these weak points fast enough to keep it out. She feels it begin to start, like something spinning at higher and higher speed, so she pulls the van to the side of the road. She braces for the attack, as if this will help. She forgets to reach above her head and turn the camera off.

Mastering the braking system was an exercise in prosthesis, in the knowing of delay. Unmasterable. You're in the head of a long, many-thoraxed creature, whose joints are made of lag and imprecision. Now, on-board computers handle this. But were this train driverless, could it have gone otherwise? Would an automated subway car have known to stop, have tried to stop at all? But an automated train wouldn't experience the mental and visual fatigue that made this possible. What happened wasn't just a possibility, though, but an inevitability, wasn't it? She repeats this to herself: it was someone's decision other than your own, something outside of your control. Something executed faster than reaction time could comprehend, faster than any reflex, let alone one mediated by a hundred feet of trailing machine, could respond to. Or could you have, if you weren't so tired, if you weren't trying so hard not to think? No, even fatigue, even a kind of meditation, can't be at fault. And neither can you. Your eyes were on the track, were looking where they were supposed to be looking. At that point you didn't even need to glance down at the controls. You had already started to slow the train down, slowly, but maybe if it hadn't been so slowly, if you had already scrubbed off enough speed by that point—then, again, that was what you were supposed to be doing, avoiding a jolting, harsh stop. Although that came. It was you, you were there. But a driverless train would have done no better, would have slowed down just the same, if not slower, and in fact would not have even tried to stop. It wouldn't have seen him come out from the far side of the column.

The feeling is like a kind of acceleration inside her, a keening and rising sheet of nausea. *You did*, she tells herself. *You did see*. The station was underlit and there was a crowd on the platform but you did see him, at the last moment, ten or fifteen feet away, as he came out from behind the column, out of the shadow. No one else noticed him, not so much running as striding, stepping out—but you did see him, knew what you were seeing right away, or thought you did, but by then there was so little distance in front of the subway car. He had done this on purpose, picked a spot as close as possible to the station's opening and the train's top speed. And the old magnetic brakes. A newer train, not just fully automated but with double-locking brakes on every car, with electronic instead of just electric braking, would have stopped in time. But it would not have known to stop. And if it did, it would have scattered its passengers, all two hundred of them, down the aisle, some, especially the young, old, infirm, sustaining serious injury, if it would have stopped.

This logic is too abstracted, too hypothetical, to work. She tries it every time and it doesn't slow anything down. Nothing works. But she tries it again: if the brakes were new and you stopped in time it would have been just as bad. You felt it yourself. You hit the brakes as hard as you could, wrenching the lever back towards you so hard that the steel handle bent flat to the console. And it wasn't a sudden stop, not as sudden as it needed to be, but sudden enough that it sent you into the windshield of the conductor car just as he was crushed into it from the other side. You fell back into your seat, but he went underneath. *You did see him. You did.*

The silence of the van, punctuated by the clicking of the camera. The sound of her breathing, and of the body going under.

CHAPTER TWO

WHEN WIN TAKES THE CALL, SHE SWIVELS herself away from her workstation, and, feet kicking, propels herself into an empty cubicle at the far corner of the room. She does this less out of a presentiment of what the call means, than out of a subconscious urge towards privacy that is probably, along with her burgeoning face blindness, the number one side effect of this job. Win does have some inkling of alert; it's six o'clock, near the end of the day for drivers, but Ana should still be in her van, clicking away on some boring demi-urban road somewhere. She never calls during her shift; she's too busy driving in that weird intent way she does. Win's only had a few calls from her during work hours and, well: this is the first sign.

In the creepy cubicle—so called because, even though vacant for almost a year now, there are still loads of photographs pinned to its felted interior, photographs not like Win's printout gallery of strangers and oddities, but photos of family members whose relationship to the long-gone scrubber can only be guessed at—Win pulls off her headset and puts the phone—her cell phone, and not the company line, which is another sign—to her ear.

For the first few minutes of the phone call, Win's gaze is locked with a photograph of a young girl, teenage or college-aged, but for once, she's not wondering who this person is—daughter? girlfriend?—but is instead holding this gaze as a kind of surrogate, without thinking, the eyes in the photo standing in for the eyes of her friend, for the visual, if not physical, contact that the moment needs. Ana's words aren't coming out clear, but Win knows what is happening; even knowing what is happening, she is straining, struggling to make things out. It's not easy; it's mostly just bits and pieces of language, the air not coming in fast enough to form them. Win speaks through the gaps:

"Are you in the van?"

"Are you pulled over?"

"Are you close?"

Win has known about these episodes for close to a year, has been privy to, witness to, a handful, some through the phone, some in person, though fewer. She has heard the story, after having put it together from the parts offered up in these moments; she at first knew only of some horrible presence that would enter and exit Ana's life, following its own course, triggered and then dormant, resting for months and then consuming entire days. It was months into the closest chapter of their friendship before the thing itself was revealed. Win had known it obliquely, as some trauma or catastrophe, but had misjudged the narrative. Someone had hurt her friend, she thought, someone who she loved and trusted had done some terrible thing that had hurt both her and trust itself, making the act of sharing impossible. A friend who had killed friendship. When she had finally heard the story, after a weekend away at a beach someplace whose three-day span was haunted by that thing, a darkening presence so obvious that Win had finally grabbed Ana and asked her for the love of God to tell her what was happening or what had happened, and she had told her, the horror of it had been so great that it was her, Win, who had needed to be comforted.

The last day of the trip, a holiday Monday, they didn't leave the house, but stayed in, stayed at the same table, from morning coffee to the last grainy sip of rummaged-up merlot, and if the thing wasn't in the conversation it was behind it, something that filled every sentence spoken and gave it the weight of both grief and a new and powerful closeness. And when Win dropped her off at her apartment the next day, there was something in their goodbye, in her look, that suggested that something had been transferred from one to the other, even if it must return to its host to sleep.

Win's eyes are still stuck on those of the photograph, but she's not really looking now. She's listening to the voice on the other end, trying to measure the situation, trying to figure out whether she should stay on the line or run to her car and find the spot on the map where the van was parked. She has learned the things to say and is saying them, repeating them, insisting on them, in the spaces between when she has time to speak. When those spaces grow too large — when Win realizes that there is silence on the other end, and that there has been this for a few minutes now, and all she can hear is her own voice, saying whatever it is that she can think to say—she curses herself and runs down the fire escape, taking the steps three at a time.

By the time she reaches the van, after nearly getting lost in the same industrial grid, it's dark. As she pulls to the side of the road there is a blinding flash, and then another, and another: the rig, left on, going off in its steady three-second interval. The cameras track Win, her approach illuminated in stop-motion bursts. She'll see them the next day, overdue in her inbox, and has the eerie experience of wiping her own face smooth. First flash, first picture: she's between the two cars, caught in the middle by the burst of light. Picture two: she is along the side of the van, hand outstretched to keep balance on the loose gravel shoulder. The light catches her again, now with the passenger door half open, grabbing hold of the van's roof to pull herself up into the cabin. Flash: then she's gone, the door shut. The camera fires once more, then is turned off.

Win hangs up and takes a look at her friend in the driver's seat. She takes Ana's swollen face, lit up by the dashboard lights, in her hands, talks to her, conveys her presence in as many ways as she knows how. She says her name, softly, and it's the only sound. She says it again, and again, until Ana's eyes meet hers, and her friend returns.

CHAPTER THREE

WIN DOESN'T REMEMBER WHEN SHE started keeping an eye on the away postings on the company's listserv, but it had become part of her morning routine. She'd arrive at work at around ten—it didn't matter so much when the she got there, only that her shift ended after those of the drivers so that she'd have time to process the last of the day's images—and, after refilling her travel mug and grabbing some of whatever catered breakfast there was left, she would boot up her workstation and check the dailies. In there with the inter-office memos and links to press releases would be postings, once in a while, of short-term work available at other sites—usually to fill in temporary vacancies, sometimes to meet spikes in the demand for imaging when a city's real estate market exploded. A scrubber in Palo Alto had a baby, two or three years ago, and Win filled in, coming back five months later with a good tan and a taste for farm-to-table cuisine, both completely unsustainable here.

But most of the time, Win was keeping an eye out for driver gigs. She managed to land Ana one of the first overseas postings, got her it as a kind of birthday gift. Win couldn't go with her, but she was happy imagining her friend winding her way through the concentric maze of Amsterdam, a nightmare for tourists and a total dream spot for her. This was shortly after their actual trip together, when Ana confessed her need for difficulty, for distraction. Win made it her personal duty to throw as much of this her way as she could. It was Win who gave her the idea of turning off the nav screen, or rather unplugging it from behind, something Ana never thought of. This was technically sabotage of company property, but as long as she remembered to plug it back in before she turned the van in, well, who would be the wiser? Some of the other drivers found out, but they chalked it up to eccentricity and didn't step in. Most of them, who drove more through the screen than through their windshields, were just impressed that she never got lost.

Win's sitting in her cubicle; it's the end of the shift, and Ana is waiting with her as she finishes the last set of the day. It is two weeks after the incident outside of the industrial complex. Ana went back to work the next day and Win knew better than to push her to take time off. Instead, the listserv. Win's clicking through emails, mostly inter-office stuff, which either goes over her head or pay scale or beyond her attention span because she deletes them as soon as they load. Ana's not looking at the screen, and she's not on her phone either, but is, instead, just zoning out. Win shift-clicks a chunk of administrative stuff and it scuttles into her trash bin. The next email in the queue opens.

"Hey, Ana."

"Yep."

"Look, check out this one." She double-clicks the message so it opens full-screen and leans to the side. Ana wheels over.

"Another away job?"

"Yeah, why not? Here, here's the best part." Win scrolls down.

"A driver, and a scrubber? That's all they need?"

"That's us. Let's do it."

"When?" Win scrolls back up.

"It's a Friday to Friday gig, two weeks from now."

"That works."

"Yeah? I can make it happen if it's good for you."

"Yeah, that works."

"Where is this place?"

CHAPTER FOUR

ANA'S APARTMENT IS ON THE FOURTEENTH floor and has windows in half the rooms, and those rooms that are without windows still have curtains. She's not sure what to do with them, whether she should keep them drawn or parted, or simply take them down. She's also not sure what to do with the outcropping of plaster in the corner of the main room, a kind of vestigial fixture from the suite's past. A capped and painted-over pipe sticking a few inches from the bottom of the enclosure suggests it once was a gas fireplace. The pipe keeps her from putting anything on the floor of the opening, and common sense keeps her from tampering with the pipe. At the top of the protrusion, where the fireplace—if that's what it was—met the wall, is a flat space, like a mantle, but angled such that anything placed on top of it would fall onto the floor. If she owned the apartment she'd tear the thing out of the wall, sand it smooth, paint it over, finish the job of erasing it that had been started decades ago. Instead, she tries to ignore it.

It's the late evening; Win has just dropped her off at home after giving her a ride from the office punctuated by a stop at a drive-through window for dinner. They ate in the parking lot of her apartment building, watching the windows illuminating one at a time, the lights turned on and off in each room by the push of a button from the smartphone Ana held in her free hand. Win sensed that Ana was burnt out and didn't ask to come up. They side-hugged over the centre console, Ana grabbed the wrappers and paper bags, crouched out of the car, then watched Win reverse out onto the road. She flashed the apartment windows one more time: *good night.*

Ana's laptop screen coats the apartment's interior with blue light as she scrolls through search results, maximizing and minimizing pages. She's already said yes to Win and submitted her application, because of her friend's insistence and because she knew that she was right, that maybe she needed this: so now she's doing research. Not maps, as that would rid the situation of its novelty and blunt the purpose of the away job, but general information, historical, geological. She hadn't heard of the island before, only the name of its cluster, and had been to none of them even though they were only a three-hour drive, plus ferry ride, from the city. Despite this proximity, the island, Peliatos, bore little relation to the metropolis. It was a rocky crag, wild and forested, its shores and cliffs buffed smooth by the ocean. Its population was a scant four hundred, growing to over a thousand twice a year as the leisured middle class from surrounding cities fled the extreme inland summer and winter for its mild, ocean-buffered climate. The biannual influx helped the economy but otherwise had small impact on the culture of the island, which was in the majority occupied by the children of the recluses who made their way over in the sixties. That was, of course, only the two most recent sets of migrants to the island. The hippies and retirees followed a pattern that had been articulating itself over the span of centuries.

Peliatos—the name sounded Latinate, or possibly Greek, but it arrived at this through the distortion particular to territories that changed hands, and languages, many times over.

Fernando Manera y Pilatos was twenty-six years old when he received his commission from the kingdom of Spain to sail to the New World and, upon arriving, to stake out land for his country. It was 1782, late for seizure of new territory in the Americas, so Fernando was sent to the furthest extent of the continent, the West, charting a laborious and wasteful course around Cape Horn during which half of his crew fell so ill as to be useless. He arrived in present-day California, and sailed north of the forty-ninth parallel as ordered. When he reached his destination, he saw, contradicting his briefing, fires burning on the shore, presumably British or French trappers who had beat his ship on foot. He thought better of forming a greeting party, and instead continued northward into worsening weather, a vanishing sun, and an increasingly hostile geography, until his ship was enveloped on both sides by a scattering of small islands wet with rain and black-green with vegetation. No fires were burning. At the largest of these islands, he ordered his crew to draw the ship ashore. It was night, and the men refused to board the dinghies, so Pilatos and his crew slept on deck in the overwhelming quiet, scattered among the expedition supplies, with the island and its unknown inhabitants sleeping beside them. The sun rose on a shore glittering with billions of pulverized shells, a beach that ran up against a dense, lightless forest, a wall of evergreen that towered over the ship at two and three times the height of its masts. Pilatos and the members of his crew well enough to form an excursion paddled into a bay perfectly sheltered by sandstone banks that were carved by tidal action into great mirrored waves of rock. There they tied up their boats and vanished into the woods, returning two days later, having seen no living souls, declaring the island cleared for their purposes by God, toting strange new berries, butchered game, and a few sacks of what could have been gold. The return of the exploratory party to the ship, the *Santa Maria,* was well attended—it was watched by those waiting aboard the ship and, from a vantage point directly opposite, by a large group of the island's actual inhabitants who stood in the shelter of the forest. They had watched the men come to the shore, had studied them as they plucked and pillaged, but out of caution did not interfere. Pilatos left behind a small group of men whose spirits were buoyed by the bounty whose surface they had only just scraped; they left the island they had joyously named after its discoverer, and promised speedy return with an enlarged crew and stowage.

Pilatos was never to return to the island; his successes earned him a better, more lucrative position as an administrator in the homeland. The subsequent expedition, sent out the following year, in the same boat and with some of the same crew, returned to the fledgling colony to find it mysteriously empty. The settlers' camp, made near the beach of Esperando Bay, was intact, but abandoned; the second group fought their feeling of unease and took up lodgings there, and, like their predecessors, waited to see what would happen. It was months until the Spaniards were able to forge a path up the cliffs that separated their southeastern sliver of the island from the rest, and from atop this plateau, they saw the wild waves of the Pacific Ocean spreading out past the green mass of the island— the edge of which was, their accounts confess, much further away than anticipated—and, below, revealed by the plumes of smoke and clearings of felled trees, the villages of the island's original inhabitants, the size of which spoke to a population of thousands. The settlers made a hasty return down the cliffs to their own small outcropping of island, boarded their ships, and left, planning to return with an entourage large enough to initiate a trade outpost, or failing that, to wipe the island clean.

They ended up doing both. Within thirty years of its introduction to European settlers, the island's original culture was wholly erased through a land treaty, originally abstract, but one that was enforced by increasingly concrete, and violent, means. A century passed, by which time the British took complete control of the mainland and the descendents of the original Spanish settlers fled, either south into California or all the way back to Spain. Through the slackness of orthography, Isla de Pilatos became Pelatos Island, and then, through a final aberration, Peliatos Island. At the tail end of the nineteenth century, a successful quarry and brickworks were founded, and the tiny landmass had a brief industrial flourishing that was cut short in 1898 by the discovery of coal deposits on neighbouring Skathis Island. Industry left Peliatos and never really returned, leaving behind a few traces in the impossibly rectilinear shelves of sandstone on the northern end of the island and the occasional brick tripped over by a wading vacationer. When they bent to pick up the stamped-clay block, or ran their hands over the ragged sandstone edge hacked out by pickaxes that now mouldered in the seabed, they'd respond to these remnants in the same way they'd react to the petroglyphs carved into the cliffs a thousand years earlier. It was the same feeling that their predecessors, those Spanish settlers, were programmed to feel: the disbelief that anyone could have been here before, a readiness and need to believe that they were treading on virgin, untouched land. It all seemed to Ana like a colossal yet blind short-circuit of history, the tape of empire twisted into a Möbius loop and fed back into the machine to erase and rewrite the same sequence over and over again.

Industry left; money didn't, at least not for long, nor did the mythos of excursion, of the paradise at the end of the continent. Peliatos was, as the satellite images showed, far from the westernmost island of its grouping, but it was easiest to get to, had the most dramatic landscape and an unbroken view of the Pacific, and so was deemed by those who benefited from such pronouncements as the rough and romantic end of the earth. Or was in the process of being so deemed. This, Ana imagined, attracted a certain kind of individual, one for whom the end of the world presented an attraction that was as fatalistic on a universal level as it was heroic on an individual one. And these certain kinds of individual, or at least their spending power and their ability to create market trends, attracted her employer, and sent her and Win, expenses paid, to do some exploring of their own. Another advance party; another excursion. One more pass through the tape head, Ana thinks to herself, and clicks her laptop shut.

Ana knows why she dropped out. She didn't tell her mother, but it wasn't because she had no answer. And her silence was not because she was embarrassed, guilty, but because she recognized in advance that communication would be impossible. How could she explain to her mother, who thought she built computers—built, materially, by hand, in silicon and metal—what made her leave? Her mother, who never understood her work? The functioning was higher, higher levels of complexity, plasticity, implication, than she could grasp. Ana could grasp them, and she was afraid. She sat in seminar rooms rigid with primal dread. *Afraid of computers?* Her mother's voice.

They had to pick one of three program streams early; Ana picked machine learning. Partly because of a fascination with artificial intelligence, with the stacking and accretion of the building blocks of protocol and behaviour and self-awareness—things that, if she was honest with herself, the computer could do better than she could—and partly because the idea appealed to her in an applied sense. She wanted technology to provide a kind of grace. She thought the purpose of these devices and programs was to fabricate, or at least simulate, ease, fluidity. She had a fantasy of the twinning of user and program, a mutual reaching or bridging, each learning and adapting to the other. A seam that would grow seamless, smoothed flush by a collaboration that grew at exponential speed. And then she went to class for four years and had all of this removed from her, evacuated and replaced with a nauseous fear. The monetizing undercurrent of the program, the department, steered discussion towards market prediction and consumer responsiveness. This made sense: there was no money in cyborgs. It was an education in algorithms, which she expected, but what she didn't expect, didn't want, was that this imagined convergence between human and program could become something perverse and dark. It wasn't the expansion of human possibility, but the opposite, the contraction of human choice into a narrowing field of "predictables."

As a child, Ana used to have nightmares, episodes of panic that would form at the end of dreams and grow upon waking into a state of overwhelming, paranoiac terror. It was always the same. Something would come to her, surfacing in her sleeping mind. It presented itself as a number, an integer, that she was bound up with in an inescapable and inconceivable pact. She had to do something with this number, something that would affect, hurt, even erase, others. It was a dark quantity, visual, outside of measure, yet somehow, she knew, it was growing. It emitted like exhaust bits of integers, factors, ratios, intimations of scale that racked her with nausea. It would take her with it, or she would take them, everyone, with her. The number was years, decades, centuries, moving in reverse like a vast erasing stylus. It was a cliff that she was at the edge of, an ocean on top of her, the maximal terror of outer space—an infinity that was somehow doubling with each turn of her thoughts. She would try to block it from her mind, but it was her mind, had taken over her mind and turned it into an exponentially unfolding black sheet of dread. There was nothing outside of it. It was something she had to do, even if she didn't want to, and it was happening, now. She'd sit upright and rocking at the foot of her bed, or walk through the halls and into different rooms, trying to get away from it, but it grew with every breath until it was large enough to envelop her, swallow the world, the matter of existence itself. It would turn everything into nothing, she would do this, and she couldn't stop it. When it was with her she wouldn't think of finding someone, her brother or sister in the next rooms, or calling a friend. The sheer quantity overran sense, and it would have to run its course. When her parents found her she would be curled around the base of the sink, or lying at the bottom of her closet, or standing in the pantry, saying over and over again in a whispered voice that she was sorry.

And then one day, the nightmares stopped.

The last time it came to her, she was a teenager, passing the night in a friend's garage with around a dozen others, most of them kids that her parents would have never let her spend time with. She had drifted off amid the mumbled talk and music and woke up, knowing immediately what it was, feeling the dense liquid blackness welling up in her from the vacuum of the dream. She knew she had to leave before she couldn't hide it from the others. She got out of the garage, ran to the back door of the house, and into the first room she could find. She held onto the bathroom counter and stared into her reflection, trying to will the thing out of her, but it didn't work. Her eyes, buried in dark red eyeshadow, wouldn't hold focus. She got down onto the floor and pushed her back against a wall and stayed as still as she could until it was over. Hours spent like this, frozen, while it cascaded over her. Then she went back to the others, back to her spot on the floor. When the morning light came and it was clear she wasn't going to fall asleep she walked home, had a shower, turned seventeen, graduated high school, cut her hair, moved out, and went to college.

What started the nightmares? There was a book she read as a child, something fantastical, about a high-school hero facing his archnemesis, an evil genius with a plan to stop time. He would activate the mechanism and, first, years would repeat, then months, then weeks. People would go about their business, unaware—their memories would be repeating, too, wiped clean with each interval, without even the suspicion of déja vu. Then each day would, at its finish, start over again, each iteration losing some small unit of time, a minute, a second, until the loop had tightened to a few hours' length. Then an hour, and less, fifteen minutes, one minute, ten seconds, two, and then, at the end, just a single sliver of time—a nano-second or some unit even smaller, a molecular instant, the space between start and end so fine as to not exist. The loop would scream and spin into eternity at its obliterating pitch, the entirety of existence trapped within it.

Ana thinks it might be this feeling that the dream is about, but there are times when she thinks that that the dream came first and the book came after. The dream, then the book, then the algorithm, each confirming what-ever dark thing was behind them all.

It was a final assignment, halfway through the pro-gram. Adaptivity. If you were this far along, you were good, and the seminar had them recreating from scratch the code implemented in backroom servers by the titans of social media. How to have users choose what to see with-out choosing, how, in the flash between thinking and act-ing, experience and preference, to intervene. Something in this, in the code itself, disturbed her. She had thought that human choice, at base inconsistent, would always mud-dle the algorithm, introduce inefficiencies. Seeing the raw particulars of the code, what it wanted to be and where it wanted to go, told her otherwise. Every choice the user made delivered two kinds of information, positive and negative preference, and these could be used to winnow out items likely to be preferred. User chooses a, instead of b, which indicates that they are more likely to prefer a^1 to a^2. De-emphasize a^2 and other items related through term association. Wait for the next selection, and use this to further refine the model. With each individual statement of preference, the algorithm was able to eliminate a set of items unlikely to be chosen, and in doing so retroactively validate its own judgment: the choices were not important, for they were not chosen. Most of what isn't chosen isn't seen—the choice is made for you, by an extension of your own taste. This was the original appeal for Ana, but in the asymptotical logic that she found in the code, *code she had written herself*, the mechanism revealed its abhorrent drive. She saw the teleology, the determined outcome, the end point: the range of options exponentially reduced to a vanishing point. In its naked state, the code revealed that what it really wanted to do was to close the window of reality, to draw it narrower and narrower, each consecutive choice screened and selected until each person saw just one thing, over and over, for the rest of their lives. The nightmares came back.

CHAPTER FIVE

WIN AND ANA ARE ON THE FERRY, OR, really, in the van on the ferry. They've got a good spot, right up near the front, and could get a nice picture with the camera rig if they wanted to bother turning the system on. The ferry is a big floating upright U, the middle being the vehicle deck and on both sides an enclosed seating area that they'll probably explore once the boat starts moving. Their view, hemmed in by the cabins on either side, is a picture postcard, an advertisement for the chain of islands that the ferry will be hopping between for the next hour and a half. Peliatos Island is second on the itinerary. Win tries to imagine the hassle of living on the fifth island and having to get to work in the morning, but figures that the kind of person who'd move to the fifth and smallest island in an already remote archipelago wouldn't have a day job on the mainland, if even a job at all. Parked behind and around them is a whole army of construction equipment: diggers, drillers, backhoes, and a towering machine that looks like it might be for digging wells or punching in foundations.

There are only a few non-commercial passengers on the ferry, and, parked in their old Saab coupes and beaten-up station wagons, the locals look pissed off and dismayed that they're sharing a ride with the weapons of industry. The machines do seem particularly military-industrial, immaculate yet threatening; they're fresh out of the box, their safety-orange paint not scuffed up at all, and their digging implements look brand new, unused. Win supposes that will change soon enough, and wonders what island they're heading towards to hack up and renovate.

In the back of the van, stuffed in among the spare lenses and replacement rig parts, is their luggage. The trip is only six days, so they've packed light: a sleek-looking rolling suitcase, belonging to Ana, and a duffle bag that Win now digs through, twisted around in her seat, until she finds her old Pentax and pulls it out. She uses up one of the fifteen remaining exposures on a shot out the windshield, in case they don't have postcards on the island. The ferry engine turns over with a impact strong enough to rock the van on its suspension, and, with a thunderous roar, they are in motion. Win slings the camera around her neck and gets out, stretching against the side of the van as the wind buffets against her. Ana joins her at the front, and they move off together, swaying with the motion of the ferry and wind, towards the starboard passenger cabin.

The·noise is somehow louder in here, loud enough to make conversation impossible, so the two walk the length of the cabin without speaking. A display rack bolted to the wall holds dozens of informational flyers advertising a hundred tourist-type activities to be done on the islands. All of the flyers stuck into the flap labeled Peliatos are for surfing schools, surfboard rentals, surf shops, the whole island apparently one big surfing monoculture. Win's never surfed, and she's not going to try learning in January, no matter how thick the wetsuit is. Ana touches her arm and points to a bank of seating next to a window, through which the water bouncing off of the hull looks frothy and scary-cold. Win takes a picture before sitting down, window seat. When she tries to rest her head against the Plexiglas the rumble of the engines makes her teeth clank together.

Outside of the window the islands, ghostlike and dark in the mist, come into closer view. They lie low to the water like barges, except for one, whose outline on the nearest shore rises quickly into a flat, shaved-off plateau, like a bad haircut from the eighties. Ana looks up from her phone.

"That's it, I think."

"Cool." Win leans forward in her seat to fast-forward her view. "We're recording all over that thing?"

"Yeah."

"Hard to think there's that much to see."

Ana shrugs in response, a kind of *who knows* shrug, and sits forward in her seat, too, now that Win is blocking her view. They watch together as the island slides past in the distance. The moment it leaves their window, the ferry operator announces the first stop, which sounds like Stasis Island but couldn't possibly be. They walk up the narrow staircase and emerge on the viewing deck to watch the disembarking cars, of which there are only two, unload. Nobody gets on. When the ferry backs out of the dock and enters the waterway, the wind is more intense than the speed of the sluggish ferry can explain, and they hang onto the railings and grin into the gusting salt-infused air. Ahead of them, Peliatos is a big, black and green mass, dotted with white specks of houses and docks that multiply as they get closer. It's a quick trip after the first island, and the operator announces the next stop before warning that he's going to blast the horn and then blasting, *blasting* that horn. Win and Ana run down to the van, ears ringing, and ride out the last few minutes in their seats. The harbour comes into view—larger than the one on the first island, but still tiny, a little cabin-like building that dispenses the tickets, a three-lane holding area, and the dock itself, its two widespread arms padded with truck tires. The ferry slows down, its engine working hard, and bumps itself into port. A woman comes out with a safety vest on, pulls back the gate, and stands by while a similarly dressed man on the other side lowers a drawbridge that falls onto the deck with a bang. In the rear-view mirror, the digger and excavator operators climb into the cabins of their machines and buckle their five-point harnesses. For all appearances they, the operators, Ana, and Win, are part of the same crew, and they basically are—as Ana would say, they're just different ends of the same process. The van has its own particularly military vibe, and looks, in relation to the big diggers, like some kind of scout. They're all in it together, it seems, but this doesn't keep the men from honking and yelling when the van takes a second to start.

Ana switches on the camera rig the moment their tires hit pavement. The plan is to do the main highway, the one that rings around the entire island, now, and then on the way back around check into the hotel that is a few min-ute's drive in the opposite direction. If there's any light left, they'll do a quick tour of the immediate area, but that's unlikely, and Win would rather that they just get dinner and a drink and hang out in the hotel sauna. The only place of accommodation whose booking process was offi-cial enough to bill to the company was surprisingly swank: a newly built waterside resort with a full spa, an indoor pool, and compulsory room service. Ana says she can get the driving done in four days, giving them three days to explore the island, relax poolside, and in general live like gods on the company dime.

The road from the ferry terminal is smooth, recently tarmacked, but as soon as the harbour vanishes from sight the road surface drops its guise and degrades into choppy, acne-pocked chaos. After five or so minutes of this, they come to a fork in the road where the highway—if one could really call it that—confronts the butt end of the plateau, and splits to wrap around both sides of the island. Ana turns the van right and follows the road as it cuts through back to the coast. Despite the hammering on the van's suspension, Win has to admit, it's beautiful, the road cutting through the towering old-growth forest, cedar, sequoia, with the light coming in snatches through the tree cover. She can't hear the clicking of the camera over the rumble of the tires, and checks to make sure it's on—maybe it's been rattled off its mount already, smashed on the side of the road, and they'll have the whole week to themselves. Alas, no, the status light is green, the array doing its job of taking a three-hundred-and-sixty-degree photograph every few seconds and sending it through the fibre optic cable into the memory banks bolted to the floor of the van. The road curves back to the left and levels out, and now, between the trees, Win can see water, ten or so feet down from the road, glinting in the sun, waves washing up on a thin beach, and in the distance, the mainland.

AN HOUR LATER, THE ROAD HAS PULLED BACK FROM the shore and is buried in trees. Win's on her phone, reading the island's Wikipedia page out to Ana, who's read it but lets her go on anyway. Win has learned on her own that the island is big; they haven't reached the northernmost tip yet. To their left, across the facing lane, the ground rises in a ridge of pushed-up rock, a little higher than the roof of the van; beyond it, Win can see more trees, and she knows from maps that past these are the last few miles of the cliff face, the plateau, before it drops back down to ground level, but the forest is too dense to see anything. They keep going in and out of service, and the dot on Win's smartphone map has been jumping around, first lagging and skipping along the highway, and then winking in and out of existence entirely, reappearing in the centre of the island, disappearing, and then dropping them right in the middle of the channel. For the past little while, turnoffs to the left have been passing by, entrances to the crazy maze of roads they'll be winding through soon enough. A road sign, the first in forever, informs them that they're approaching the scenic viewpoint at the island's pointed end. They take a few minutes' break, Win uses up a couple more shots on her roll of film, and then they're back in the van and Ana is switching the rig back on.

The west side of the island, at least from the road, is not much different. Again the long sections of busted rock piled up to the left, here and there a road forking off inland, and the forest to the right, with the occasional driveway and, where the trees are thin enough, glimpses of water, this time stretching all the way out to, Win figures, Japan. The ocean this side of the island looks much rougher, and they can see whitecaps between the trees, but the trees are the same, the ferns sprouting up at the bases of the trees the same, even the ramshackle mailboxes at the ends of the dirt driveways, for all of their DIY quirkiness, eventually seem identical. Win is surprised at how quickly her wonder can turn into boredom. She's even stopped noticing the pits and potholes in the road. Ana looks bored, too, though it's hard to tell, since she's looking straight ahead at the road, hands low on the wheel, fingers flexing open and closed, in time to something, though there's no music on. Win looks back to the road and at that moment there is a streak of something, beige, or grey, that flickers out from Ana's side of the windshield, and this is all in a second, and Ana screams, the van veers hard right, and there's a split second of weightlessness, and then Win blacks out.

CHAPTER SIX

IT STARTS WITH THE TIDAL PATTERN—THE
monthly highs and lows, then daily, the ocean's retreat
around noon, its return in the evening, to stay overnight, coming in on slow, liquid, pulses, the beat between
rolling, peaking, subsiding, rows of waves sloping towards
the shore—waves making up, fold by fold, the tide, each
adding its wax and wane to the growing, rising median—
and on each wave, between each, creases of water, ripples,
each with its own groove and furrow, crest and trough,
zenith and nadir. Waves inside of waves inside of waves,
from lunar breathing to subatomic rhythm, cosmic to ele-
mental, universal to particular.

But it is not so simple, so harmonious as that.
Underneath the basic equation of peak, trough, period, and
phase, a dark factor, a third variable, enters, rising up from
the blackness of sea depth. Its presence is incremental, a

fraction of a fraction of influence at first, a minute shifting of interval. It stays this way for a million, a hundred million iterations, before it starts its slow ramping upwards. It evidences itself in a tightening, a surface aggression, as the space between peaks begins to close. Cycles of current, dragged into motion against the rising floor, spiral up cogwise into larger and larger units of force. Above, the stacking of microscopic swell, fold, ripple starts, ever subtly, to rake. The languid bottomless roll grows edges, begins to shift from a toothless sinusoidal arc into something with curl and tension.

On the water's topmost layer, intrusions of chaos shiver the grooves into joined and split veins of turbulence. Five, ten miles out from the shore, the shelf accelerates its rise, crushing columns of tumbling water upwards, the wavelength shortening, contracting at an exponential rate. The drag of wind on the ocean's roughened surface and the rushing-up of the seabed turn the waves gradually sawtoothed, their windward faces pulled in, nearly vertical, into cliffs made opaque by the thick whirl of water, a sage-green freezing wall, until the moment when all this potential is made kinetic and hundreds of tonnes of matter leap up, undercut, to crash down upon the breakpoint in a cataclysm of foam.

Again, and again, and again, in horizontal bars of whitewater, spreading from edge to edge of the bounded rectangle of her window. A sky-mirroring sheet of light in the morning, a saturated, luminol blue by midday, and at night a deep evergreen cut by ash-grey breakers. Lena sits on the rattan couch and watches the changes in the tide, proofs to structures and tables she could dictate from memory.

She once lived in a cabin built high on a steep rock face, a summit whose approach was made on double-track, over river crossings of recycled wood narrower than the body of a car, across sections of loose shale. The difficult topography might have suggested solitude, but back then she was never alone. Now she lives at sea level, among the rest of the island, the common road cutting through the woods just behind, and is alone always. She has given up that other home; she has abandoned her widow's walk.

It is morning, the ocean a hard, white, opalescent skin over the secrets of the world, and she rises to move through the one-floor house, passing through rays of light that are almost completely horizontal. The water becomes coffee as she waits, holding the empty cup in her hands, still painful, feeling the lack of warmth, the lack of the prednisone she must wait to take with food. This hour, with the tides of heat and light yet to come pulsing in, with the coldness of the rooms before the hands are able to make fire, has the stillness of something brittle.

There's no snow, snow never falling on the island, but the pulverized shells of the beach stand in for snow as they stand in for sand in the summer. The shells, skeletons of molluscs, horseshoe crabs, and oysters, are largest and most intact where they are furthest from the pound of the surf. Where the tide is now lapping in, the fragments are ground so impossibly, and uniformly, fine, that they seem not only inorganic but man-made, sparkling in the diffuse morning sun like cubic zirconia fresh from the mill.

Her lifelong study encompasses, too, these border zones, liminal spaces along which the sea swells and recedes, leaving them coated in its calciferous scales. She has learned the names for each kind of fragment, can reconstruct the whole from a shard of mother-of-pearl, but what is interested in her, and follows her still, is in deeper waters.

Several decades ago she was initiated, in the dark of a basement seminar room, into the occult world of underwater geography. It was in an introductory lecture on gravitational action. The moon, she learned, when blasted out of the earth, left hollows in its wake, then hung suspended while its negative image filled with water—the gathering of a second, liquid version of itself that would match its waxing and waning; its twin, with lines of filiation so strong that you could read one in the other.

She enrolled in the department of marine geography, but that training, those models, she was soon to slip out of in search of something more capacious. When she surfaced years later it was from a distant spire of the discipline, connected only to the main body by, as it were, the ocean. She defended her dissertation, at the age of twenty-seven, four hundred pages on the topic of cultural oceanography, and passed with distinction. She taught at the university for two years, mostly seminars on critical wave studies, applied for travel funding for research in North America, and never returned.

In the community of castaways on the island she is unique in how little time she has spent on the mainland. When she came here first she had, in fact, not set foot on it at all, had been carried by a taxi from the airport to the ferry terminal, onto the boat, and over the crossing, so that her first step on transatlantic soil was onto this tiny out-cropping of terra firma. An annual trip across the channel, to replenish dry goods, replace worn-out clothing, to, yes, see a movie, was a necessary evil, and she spent most of it in the old Silverado truck that a neighbour sold to her in her first winter. Otherwise, the island was enough for her.

It had been recommended to her by an ex-colleague for its unique geological structure, the fan of tectonic grooves that converged onto the island, the uncanny north-south orientation of its Pacific-facing shore. He had said nothing about the people who lived on it, the hermits, hippies, and surfers, who were much of what made her stay. The waves, however, were a great part of it. She could never leave those walls of water, kneaded together by the furrows of the sea-bed to build twenty feet high, and falling, grey-green, all through day and night. She has been on the island nearly thirty years, now, and she has exhausted many things, but she has not exhausted them.

The rush of steam through the percolator, chasing the last of the boiling water through, begins the thawing of the winter morning. The shadow of the treeline has crept midway up the beach, bringing the tide with it, and with the coffee made, the quiet in the kitchen is so pure that she can hear the shells rattle as the waves pull them in.

As she sits, hands aching around the coffee mug, lis-tening to the waves, there is suddenly something else—a screech, or a scream, and then an immense mechanical violence that tears through the air behind her cabin; it is the sound of the end of the world.

CHAPTER SEVEN

NA WAKES UP WITH THE BANG OF THE AIR bag, or after. It can't be with, but that's what she remembers: asleep, and then the bang, and her vision filled with white. Something has happened to put her here, but she doesn't know what. How long has she been awake? She can still hear the explosion in her ears, and that other sound. Her arms are stuck between her head and something: the air bag. Did it go off when she was parked? The people on the ferry will be angry, with her blocking the exit. They would have to turn the ferry around and let people—let people off the other end. Are they screaming at her? The drills have somewhere to go. Disappearing at the junction, going west while they went east. So they did get off. Then why are they screaming? The road—there was something in the road trying to kill itself. Did she hit it? Is that what is crying? She tried so hard not to, she turned in time, didn't she ... No time to brake but time to turn. She missed it. She missed it this time. It's too loud in here. The newer trains would be better. Turn? Did she forget her earplugs? She pushes her head into the pillow and it deflates, just a bit, and she sees Win.

Now she's hammering her head into the air bag, clawing at the back of it with her arms, trying to take the air out of it. It's in between her teeth, but the fabric is tough. Her brain is pounding and dots are clustering in her vision but she keeps head-butting the bag, white, but speckled with pink, until it's out of her way and her forehead is hitting the horn in the centre of the steering wheel so hard it stays on. Her arms are only half there, numb, her hands bone-white, but the feeling is coming back in them and she shoves her fingers at the seat belt release and it's off of her, the belt edged with blood is going back into the seat. Over and underneath the sound of the horn Win is doing something halfway between crying and screaming and her eyes are wide open, shot with fear, and they go wider when Ana puts her hand on the leg that is somehow caught underneath the seat, which has gone all the way forward up against the dash. Ana drags herself onto the wide centre console, the nav screen digging into her back, and leans forward to hold Win in her arms and to kick the release lever with her foot. Win screams into her ear and the seat slides back. The door is crumpled in on the passenger side, the glass spiderwebbed with cracks, so Ana wraps her arms around Win and writhes both of them back onto her seat, trying to protect the leg with her own, and she's reaching behind her head and the lever works, the door swings open and she falls out with Win on top of her. They're outside. Somehow Ana is still holding onto Win, cradling her like a child, staggering knee-deep in bushes, the van behind her making its noise. Win is quiet and when Ana looks down at her and sees that the white sock on her foot is soaked through with blood, and the denim of her blue jeans is slicked with it, the spots in her vision come back. She makes herself look up, through the rows of trees, the branches, where there is a cabin, soft-edged. The door opens, and Win suddenly gets very very heavy and the weight carries Ana down to her knees, but there's no impact, and the door opens, and someone is coming out of it, a woman with white hair and an old housecoat, moving slowly, with the spots filling everything in and the blare of the van's horn going on and on like an air-raid siren.

THE WOMAN IS HELPING HER TO HER FEET. WIN IS lying in the leaves, on her side, still. The woman is saying *help me*, holding Win by her shoulders. Ana puts her arms around her. The pitch of the van's horn is falling, the sound taking on a quaver as the mechanism fails or the battery dies or as the pain boils up the nerves to the shoulder, the neck, the brain. They get her into the back seat of the truck and Ana throws up everything in her stomach onto the gravel drive. The woman is helping Ana, now, guiding her towards the front seat, saying things of urgency. She can't get up into the seat. When the woman hoists her in, they both cry out in pain. Ana's pulling the seat belt across herself, finding it by the cold of the metal of the buckle, the spring in the latch almost too much to get through. There's a carbolic taste in her mouth, a taste from her insides but foreign, mineral, inorganic, and the tendons tied between her collarbones and skull are spasming in red-hot parallel lines.

The truck starts and shakes into gear and they're reversing out of the loose driveway, spitting rocks. Ana feels the potholes in the road in her eyes. It is quiet in the cab of the old truck, and she has been repeating, for the whole time since waking up in the van, in one continuous murmur, *oh my god oh my god oh my god oh my god.* She isn't able to stop; the best she can do is to turn the volume down until it is just a movement of her lips, like a mantra. And then she's asleep, then awake, the woman's hand on her shoulder, and she understands she can't sleep, isn't allowed, so she tries to focus on the crumbling road out of the window.

Asleep again, then awake.

Out the window the pavement moves past. Every time the truck's wheels hit a pothole pain shoots up her neck and through her skull and out of her mouth. If she looks out of the corner of her eyes she can see, through the rear-view, Win on the back seat, but she can't hold this angle for long. Win is laid flat with the seat belts buckled over her, facing the seat. There are leaves in her hair. The woman says that they are almost there, but Ana doesn't know where they are going. Every few minutes the woman reaches over and puts a hand on Ana's leg and shakes her, not hard, in a cautionary way. They arrive at another cabin, a larger one. People come out of it with

wheeled contraptions, and Ana watches as Win is taken
out of the truck and laid down. When they come around
for her she is asleep, and they wake her before lifting her
out. She is strapped down, her head wedged between two
padded brackets, and the pain of this, the clarifying, light-
ning pain, takes her out of her body.

AWAKE.

They roll Ana and Win into the emergency entrance.
Ana is laid flat on her cart, but Win has both her head
and legs elevated. They're cutting her jeans off of her, or it
at least sounds like they are—Ana can't see, can only see,
if she looks down past her feet, the back of Win's head.
Something wet and balled up is passed from the stretcher.
The group pulls closer to examine, and then something is
said, and they retract in unison and someone grabs the cart
and moves it out of sight. Ana is next, the doctors circling
her, appraising. A beam of light appears, tracks across her
field of vision, does so again, hot and close in her eyes, and
Ana tries to tell them to stop but a hand is laid under her
chin and the light disappears. The ceiling starts moving
past her head, a grid of foam tile and lights, and she passes
through some kind of gateway, and then another. The cart
stops, her arm is held, there is a pinprick, a low burn, and
then a wash of warmth everywhere. The pain fades, and
for a second she is not yet asleep but in the webbed and fil-
amented threshold of sleep, and through this medium she
sends, quickly, a message to Win: *Be okay. Be okay. Please.*

ANA WAKES UP. SHE IS BEING LIFTED FROM HER stretcher to a bed. There are many hands on her, hands lifting her head by the base of her skull, hands tucking something in between her and the pillow. Whatever it is hurts her, even through the sedative, and she makes a sound; a hand falls on her forehead, and the thing comes around from either side and links into itself with a click. Somewhere down below all of this she feels the coolness of an alcohol swab, and then the pinch of a needle. Again, the rush of warmth, but this time she does not fall asleep—the pressure is too great, the plastic and rubber choking her, enclosing her, forcing her chin upwards and her shoulders down, not away from but into the pain. Slowly it fades, but she doesn't sleep. She lays there, staring up at the ceiling, unable to look anywhere else, but not really seeing anything. There are waves of nausea, either from the pain or from the painkiller, and moments where everything seems to blur, and what thoughts she has aren't connecting, but she's still there. Every wave takes her a little bit deeper, and at the lowest point time seems to stretch out long and paper-thin, and then it contracts again, and suddenly she's out of the bed, the hands lifting her up and then down into a chair. She is wheeled down a hallway and into a room where the white-haired woman is waiting. And Win, in a gown, her face drowsy. Ana is parked next to her, cannot see her, the brace forcing her to look instead at a colour photograph of a child in traction. She reaches out and Win takes her hand. She falls asleep.

When everything comes back, Ana is in the van again. No, she is in a chair, facing a screen showing an image of the ocean. The ocean, through a window. She's in someone's home, and someone is handing her a pebbled plastic cup. It's the woman from the door. She moves away. Ana hears a sound and goes to look but something won't let her. The woman reappears and Ana sees her face.

"Don't, don't," the woman says. "Try to keep your head as still as you can."

"Whiplash," Ana mumbles.

"Yes," the woman says.

"My friend."

"She is here."

"I want to see."

The woman holds the armrests of the chair, and pushes. The chair turns on its wheels and shows her a long, low couch, on which Win lays. Win is in an old sweater and sweatpants with one leg rolled up. A cast from the ankle to the knee. She gives Ana a little thumbs up. Her eyes are tired and her smile looks put on, but she's alright. She's there.

CHAPTER EIGHT

THE METAL FRAMES OF THE TWO WHEEL-chairs, tossed by the ruts of the road, strike the truck bed over and over with a resonant clang, the same sound, again and again, but with an irregular, entropic rhythm. The interior of the truck, already aged when Lena bought it, is now even more deeply patinated, all cracked and faded leatherette, the dash deep and broad and bisected by a wooden strip that would have peeled away if it was real wood. The girl, Ana, is again in the front seat, her moulded plastic neck brace between the seat's headrest and the frame of the door, and her forehead pressed against the cool window. She's asleep, even against the banging of metal on metal, by the grace of morphine, and now there's no need for jostling her awake. She is many things but she is not concussed.

The other girl, Winnifred, is in the back seat, upright, leaning forward at regular intervals to place her fingers on her friend's hair. Her fractured leg is in a thick cast, and like the other she is full of painkillers, but she is awake. Their eyes, driver and passenger, meet in the mirror, and her expression has a weight to it not flattened out by the sedatives. She's lost a pint of blood, will be in a wheelchair for a week, is riveted with metal pins and laced with stitches, but she's straining against seat belt and fibreglass to reach her friend's hair, again and again, like doing so is chasing away some horrible thing.

At the hospital it was decided that to deliver the two to their hotel, to leave them unattended, was dangerous, so Lena is driving back home with these two young women who are now, by fiat of the doctors, under her care—at least until one or both of them becomes lucid enough to arrange transport back to the mainland. She would have taken them in, or offered this, in any case. They nearly died in the bower of trees that she had planted, twenty-five years ago, to give her home privacy from the road, and something in this gives her a responsibility over them that she accepts without deliberation.

She slows down as she drives past the darkened trails of rubber, the traces of the moment at which the tires of the van passed the critical threshold and lost contact with the pavement. As they pass underneath her wheels the tracks curve out of true with the road, aiming instead over the interval of the gravel shoulder—pointing, in a sense, at *her*. At the end of this path—the tar-black lines turning, as the tires hopped off of the asphalt and onto the grassy incline, into torn patches of bleeding brown soil—is the van, half-buried in the grove of splintered trees. She passes and turns at the open gate.

The scene is waiting for them to return, in the silence of crushed metal and the long-dead horn. The gravel is too loose for the wheelchair's wheels, so after putting them just inside the entrance and activating the brakes as instructed, Lena must half-walk, half-carry the girl with the cast, slinging her over her shoulder and bearing as much of her weight as she could manage. The second girl can walk, but slowly, heavy-lidded, arm in arm, with small unsure footfalls across the ten-foot gap between the two doors. At last they are both inside, safe, rolled into the warming living room. All at once her own pain comes back to her, the aching in her joints, the morning's dose long worn off, and she considers taking one of the pills that the doctors gave her for safekeeping. Oxycodone for whiplash, paracetamol for swelling around the fracture, rarified names that feel to her almost lyrical, ambrosial, but instead she goes to the kitchen and has her second dose of her anti-arthritic with a piece of fruit.

She's not done. In the back of the drawer in her bedroom she finds an old pair of athletic pants and a hooded sweater, and returns to move Winnifred, the one with the fractured leg, onto the couch. The plaid shirt wrapped around the girl's waist is soaked with perspiration, and she struggles at the knot with her mute fingers for some time before managing to loosen it. The girl's leg is dark with bruises well above the bandages, but Lena needs to lift her foot to slip the opening of the pant leg over the cast, and can't think of any way to do it without causing pain, and must simply do it as quickly and as carefully as she can. She takes hold of the encased leg and Winnie's hand grapples at her shoulder. Lena whispers a stream of apologies while pulling the elastic cuff up and over the cast, over the blue and purple kneecap, and as far up her thigh and away from the bruises as possible. Then the second leg is on, and she needs to get onto the seat cushion to pull the sweatpants up the rest of the way and she sees, with a tightening of her chest, that the girl's face is wet with tears. She dries them with the hood of the hoodie before putting it on, and then, exhausted, sinks onto the couch beside her.

From where she's sitting she cannot see the face of the other girl, just the curves of the moulded plastic neck brace that wrap around her collar like historical costume. Lena rehearses the doctor's instructions: she must keep the brace on, all day and night, for three days, before she is allowed to remove it to eat and bathe, and then in three more days she will remove the brace and stretch twice daily following the illustrations. She's angled the chair so that Ana is facing out of the window, where the waves are falling on the white beach. The girl is making noises, trying to speak, her hands working on the padded armrests. Lena struggles her way to her feet. She is not sure what to do, so she moves to the kitchen as quickly as she can, halfway fills a cup with water from a faucet that is cold to the touch, and brings it to her. She has no idea how she will drink it. The girl is struggling to move, trying to twist her neck, the absolute last thing that she must do. Lena tells her to stop, but it's not clear that the girl hears her, so she tries again, crouching to make eye contact, afraid to touch her.

"Whiplash," the girl murmurs.

"Yes, but you are okay. You will be okay. You just need to rest."

"My friend."

"She is here, too. Do you want to see her?"

"I want to see."

Lena rotates the chair as gently as she can until Ana is facing the other girl, and then leaves them alone in the room. When she comes back, after a shower that is as hot as she can endure, the girl in the chair is asleep, her head nodded forward against the brace. Her friend is watching her through half-closed lids, or is perhaps asleep, she cannot tell. It is past midday, meaning that the sun is visible now at the top of the window, and the water is beginning to change.

From what she could understand, the two were on Peliatos for work, performing some kind of industrial reconnaissance. They must be some part of the greater forces that were reshaping the island yet again: the resort; the advertisements in the local paper; the billboards popping up like fungus; the sudden, nearly overnight, release of government lands for private speculation. She had heard of the waves of survivalists, as they called themselves, who rode the ferries from the mainland, flush with money made in e-commerce, their start-ups that peddled toothbrushes, subscription services to rarified physical goods, "athleisure." Come to buy properties and to equip them with austere concrete compounds, the new apocalypse-chic, where they'd spend their weekends waiting for the end of the world that they themselves were, without knowing it, engineering. These girls would be the cutting edge, the explorers, the prospectors. And now they were here, on Peliatos, in her living room. Lena wasn't sure how to feel about this.

IT WAS NOT UNTIL LATE THAT DAY THAT IT OCCURRED to her to get their belongings out of the van. Now, for the first time, she was able to properly look at it. Surrounded by the carnage of torn earth and shattered trees, it looked less commercial than *scientific*. There was a large fixture bolted to the roof, a triangular frame snaked with thick cables that culminated in a black, reflective sphere. There were no markings on the exterior, no branding—not even an emblem on the front grille. The van was canted over to one side in its bed of twisted fir, and Lena had to brace her foot against the side panelling to get the door open. The interior was cleared out but for the two seats and the dead screen between them and filled with what looked to her like server racks, one of which had detached on impact and spilled circuit boards and coils of fibre optic wire. She found their luggage, tossing the duffle bag out first before struggling with the hard-shell, and on one final sweep discovered an old film camera on the passenger-side floor. She did her best not to look at the blood-spattered air bags, loosely deflated against the steering wheel and dashboard.

THE OXYCODONE SEPARATED ANA FROM THE NORMAL
flow of time until two days later, when she was weaned
down to ten milligrams. She drowsed on and off, in the
chair, for Lena was afraid to move her, each time she awoke
becoming fractionally more aware, though this was coming at a cost. Her dark brow was tight with pain. She spoke,
to ask Lena her name, to try, with her and with Winnifred,
to put back together the days that she'd lost. Her friend was
still unable to walk, but was able to manage the wheelchair,
and had explored as much of the cabin as she could before
parking herself in front of the old television set. Winnifred
was the worse of the two of them, but the damage, skel-
etal and violent though it was, was physical, predictable:
a mechanical issue. With Ana, they had to reckon with
snarled nerves, battered vertebrae, the circuitry inside the
human skull. They let days pass, then a week; the safest
thing to do was sleep.

CHAPTER NINE

THE PAIN IS RISING UP AROUND THE EDGES of the medication, but she has already taken her final dose of the day, so Ana decides to have a bath instead. She's out of the wheelchair, and mobile—or at least as mobile as she can be with her neck and shoulders strapped together. She gets up from her seat in the living room, and walks past Win, who's asleep on the couch. Lena isn't there, is out in the studio behind the house, doing what it is that she does for four or five hours a day. Ana stops in front of the bathroom mirror and looks into it. The swelling on her face has gone down, but the face that is left looks or feels different in a way she can't figure out. Maybe it's the light.

She carefully reaches back to the clasp on the neck brace and undoes it. There's some resistance; the plastic has stuck to her skin. She rubs at the marks on her neck and throat, but the seams and whorls of red stay. The doctor said it's supposed to be this tight. She crouches down—*keep back chest and neck straight*—and turns on the faucet. Taking her clothing off isn't as hard as getting into the tub. She decides to wait until it's full, hoping that the water, her buoyancy, will make a difference.

Ana is standing naked in the bathroom of a near-stranger on an island that three weeks ago she didn't know existed. The oddest thing of all was that they could have gone home yesterday; they're both well enough to travel. Lena offered to give them a ride to the ferry; on the other side they could easily hail a taxi home. But they stayed. The feeling is one of waiting, but for what? First they were waiting for her to come out of her painkiller-induced haze, and now they're waiting for something else. They participate in the same daily routine: waking up in the morning with Lena, sitting at the table with her, having their coffee and toast, and then she retreats to the outbuilding, comes back for lunch, goes back to work. They go for walks along the water, each of them slowed down by their own individual pain. In evenings they cook together, or Win cooks, or they order in from the one restaurant on the island, and they talk, or listen to Lena talk. Then they go to sleep, and it is another day in which Ana hasn't decided on a course of action.

She has vague ideas about completing her job on the island, of pulling the van out of the trees and seeing if it still works. The home office has told her to take it easy and come back when she feels ready. Win is up for, she says, whatever. She's awake; Ana can hear the knock and shuffle of her moving around on her crutches in the next room. The television is turned on, and music, vapid-sounding pop stuff, is just audible behind the running water. The channel changes, and there's talking, then Win's crutches coming down, the slide of the foot, and the couch creaking as she drops back onto it. Ana turns off the faucet and gets into the tub.

Watching her friend hobble around from room to room has made her feel many things, mostly guilt and a kind of contagious, sympathetic pain, but also a definite sense of familiarity. It reminds her of something from years ago, before she met Win, before, even, the incident. It reminds her of a building way out in the suburbs where she was once with her mother; a building full of people who were all moving like Win.

HER MOTHER WAS THERE BECAUSE HER KNEE WAS coming apart. Ana was there because it was her mother's right knee, the driving one. At that time she was living in an apartment she could see her breath in and still hadn't found a job, and so she drove her mother, bussing to her house and getting her into the passenger seat, across town to the specialist's office. They talked on the way there and in doing so broke a silence three months in the making, excepting the email sent to ask for the ride.

It wasn't a hospital, but it had the off-yellow walls of a hospital, the pale blue floor of seamless linoleum, the general atmosphere. It had the feeling of a building that was built for a specific purpose; you wouldn't find the lattice-like structure of halls and offices, everything windowless, anywhere else. And its occupants: gravity-curled until they were nearly parallel with the floor, pushing and pulling themselves to and from appointments, along hallways, into and out of the elevators that outsourced their vertical movement. Moving gracefully in this space felt like an offence.

They found the door for the orthopaedist's office and checked her in. The chairs were standard office furniture, but they were elevated on a booster platform that ran the length of a wall. There were no other seats. Her mother sat down in slow motion, weight on the armrests, while Ana stood in front of her unsure of what to do. Her knee was coming apart. This was the kind of injury that came with the approach to old age: not serious, or at least not life-threatening, but something that indexed the body's decline. Things were now wearing out. Problems like these ones were mechanical, and had mechanical cures: issues with sockets, alignment, attrition, lubrication, solved by injections, therapy, the replacement of parts. Problems with a lower existential charge. Even the cane looked, if not youthful, at least active, like a piece of hiking equipment. The bigger thing was what these things, the cane, the call, meant, and the kind of problems that they were the preliminary for. As soon as Ana sat down beside her, and for the first time that day, her mother spoke.

"I don't understand what you're doing."

"What I'm doing."

"You drop out, six weeks left. Good grades, top of the class, give it all up like that."

"I wasn't top of my class." She had the whole car ride, the phone call, to talk, but she wanted to have this conversation here?

"Top, middle, bottom, whatever. You start a thing and you finish it. Do they check for grades when you do the interview?"

"I didn't want the job. I didn't want the grades."

"And you decide that now? Five years minus a month and a half to decide, and she decides now."

"I hated it the whole time. Most of the time."

"And now what. No school and no job."

"I'll get a job."

"A job without school, what would this be, flipping burgers? Coffee?"

"I'm smart. I'll find something."

"You found something. It was being a computer programmer."

"That wasn't what it was."

"You know what it is."

"It wasn't programming. It was analytics."

"Programming, analytics. You were going to work for billion-dollar companies in Silicon Canyon. And now you will make coffee in little green apron."

"I'll find something."

"How many coffees to pay off your student debt? One hundred thousand?"

"How is your knee."

"Never mind my knee. My knee is dead because I worked twice full time to pay for school."

"I paid my own tuition. I had scholarships."

"Always? Even when in kindergarten, high school?"

"They're calling you up."

"Annika, twenty-nine, almost thirty, making coffee. Steaming milk for people on way to real jobs."

Ana remembers leaving the room and being in the long hallway, each door leading to the office of a different specialist. She remembers this scene vividly because of a man who was in the hall: a man in his seventies or eighties, with an orthopaedic shoe that looked heavy, even though it likely wasn't. The carpet-dragging sole with its five-inch lift, the man's weird twisting dance upon it, slowly across the floor. He held onto the bar installed for that purpose along the entire length of the wall, broken by the doors, and when he reached the breaks he tottered through the gap in a slow, cautious shuffle. A moment of great risk.

The walls of the elevator, too, were latticed with support rails. This was a building for people for whom the facts of sitting down, standing up, walking, were shot through with peril and required great foresight, planning, infrastructure. She held the door open until the man caught up with her. On his face was a grin, the rictus smile of old age, senility, or a kind of frantic optimism—he made it.

They rode down in silence. When the elevator doors opened Ana walked down the hall, out of the automatic doors, and caught a bus at the stop down the street. She hadn't made the conscious decision to leave her mother there, but she hadn't decided not to either. She just followed the flow of traffic down the hall, hit the starred button in the elevator. When at home she emptied her pockets and found the keys to her mother's car, she realized that it was alright because she would, of course, have a spare set. Her mother had a spare everything. And, besides, it wasn't as if she could drive.

She went online and called her a cab. And a few weeks later, she had her interview at the Department of Transportation. And a year after that, the man came out from between the columns and —

CHAPTER TEN

W IN'S LEG HURTS. IT HELPS TO KEEP IT elevated, up on the couch, but not really. Her toes, peeking out from the plaster, are numb. Her armpits are sore from the crutches. Somehow this is the worst part: the armpits, really? She could take a break from using them, the crutches, but that would mean the wheelchair, which she's sick of, or just sitting on the couch, which she's getting sick of, too. So instead she trudges across the apartment, her leg hurting, then her armpits, then her leg, then her armpits, and she knees the door open and is outside in the damp winter air.

Outside the soundscape is all relaxation CD: birds chirping, waves splashing, tree branches funnelling wind. She'd usually swivel left and clomp her way to the Adirondack chairs out front, but instead, she doesn't know why, she heads for the little building along the path, Lena's studio. She never told them *not* to disturb her, after all. The going is a bit harder over the gravel, but Win manages, though the occasional misplaced crutch-end hurts like hell. At the end of the path is the squat black box, its outside daubed with something thick and dark, same as the house. At some point in her laboured approach, Lena must have heard her; the door opens and she stands in the doorway, backlit nicely by what looks like a lot of screens. She says hello with a silent *h* and stands there, waiting for Win to close the rest of the distance—which takes a while, especially since Win's good foot is in a sock and the gravel is sharper than it really should be.

There is a little daybed in the studio and Win, with urgency overriding social grace, crashes down onto it. It's not really a studio, it's more of an office. Actually, it's more of a command centre. There's a bank of computer monitors on one wall, six of them, three more than Win uses at work, and each is displaying, well it could be just a wall of numbers for how much sense they make. Most of them are doing something that looks like a heart-rate monitor, peaks and troughs and lines indicating averages. Things were moving in what looked like real time—jagged edges flattening out, going inverse, flipping back upright, all to a crazy rhythm that reminded Win of a class she took, back in her Northeastern days, on stock market analysis. What was Lena's thing? When they had talked, over breakfast, over dinner, at night on the porch with the wool blankets, she mostly asked them about themselves, about their company and their jobs, their families. There was a slight, just perceptible imbalance in the conversation, like a kind of magnetic field, that pushed away from her and kept the conversation focused on them. Whether it was their host's interest in them or instead a desire for privacy, totally understandable, Win couldn't tell. Lena sees that Win's staring at the screens, and moves out of the way.

"What is all of this?"

"Waves. Or, more so, that which happens before waves."

"Tectonics," Win suggests.

"Yes, more or less. Plate movement. These," Lena points to the topmost row of screens, "are sensors. Leftmost is a hundred kilometres on the other side of the Juan de Fuca plate, middle is a few degrees of latitude down. The one on the right is close to us, a few hundred metres or so."

"So you're measuring, earthquakes?"

"Nothing so dramatic. Vibrations, friction. Earthquakes I leave to others. Really what I am interested in is how these," pointing again to the top row, "link to these," now the lower screens.

"What are those?" They were, again, lines, but smoother ones.

"Tide charts, weather analysis, and water-level markers. Waves."

"A surfer's dream."

"Almost. This is, in sophistication, one or two steps higher than what that would look like. Our surfer friends care about waves and tides at the level of the day: do I go out or not, when do I wake up, do I go north or south, or do I just go to the Spinnaker and talk and drink beer? Is the tide full of stinging dead jellyfish, is it pink with poison algae, is there a good land-breeze or will the waves be blown out and clipped? I have the dailies but I also have projections, what the waves will be tomorrow, next week, next year. Or what they might be, based on all of this."

"They'd kill for that intel."

"They have it! Every day I put it up on the site."

"Does your work mind?"

"My work?"

"I mean, your employer, your boss, the company you work for."

"I'm self-employed," Lena says, smiling. "Or maybe the surfers are my boss. Or maybe, it's the waves?"

"So you're just obsessed, a wave-junkie, a wave-lover, like all the surfers? I like that." Win moves her crutches out of the way as Lena sits down.

"Yes, that's me. But it's not so much out of love—I'm obsessed with the wrong kind of wave for that. The 'killer' wave."

They sit quietly and look at the motion on the displays. There's a sudden uptick, a spike, and Win's heart jumps in her chest.

"Is that why you're here?"

"What—is what why I'm here?" Lena turns to Win.

"The 'Big One.' Y'know. Are you studying it?"

"I can't study it yet because it hasn't yet happened, but yes, that is part of it—I'm trying to track it, or the micro-events that would lead up to it."

"So we can stop it?"

"It can't be stopped. "

"Right."

"But we, this research, could at least provide a—I suppose you'd say, a heads-up. A window of time."

"To pack up and get out."

"Yes, if you can, if you want to."

"Want to?"

"I don't think that everyone would leave, even if we could give them enough time."

"Wait, but ... it's the apocalypse, right? Why wouldn't people want to run?"

"I don't know. It is difficult to explain, but the people who live here, many of them at least, feel like they've made a choice in coming to this island. They know that this little outcropping of land is completely exposed, that it is going to take the brunt of whatever it is that inevitably comes. And it is inevitable: it could be two hundred years from now, or ten, or in a week. It could happen right now, while we sit here talking."

"I don't like this."

"There are safety measures—sirens, evacuation points, zones of shelter and high ground—but if it is the one, the major seismic event, these will all be useless. I had a hand in developing some of these, but in truth, even I am not sure they would work. Perhaps if you were close to the inner channel, could cross it quickly; if we're lucky, the ridge might provide a breakwater, a barrier, that could protect the eastern half of the island. But the coming wave would likely wash right over it, sweeping the island bare of its forests, its wildlife, people, every trace of the built environment."

"No time to run, no time to hide."

"No, not in essence. We could give half an hour, which would be enough for the most prepared among us to reach the mainland-facing side of the island, but what then? Even if these few were able to cross the channel, if the Coast Guard could send out rescue boats in time, the vast majority would be left on the island to face the tsunami. This is all just common sense; I don't doubt that everyone on Peliatos has some version of this order of events in their mind. Or, at least, they have had this for the past fifteen, twenty years, since the 'Big One' was first theorized, its eventuality made known outside of scientific circles."

"And they stayed."

"They did not just stay. They came. Many of the current residents of Peliatos migrated here in the past decade: our young ones, come from the mainland, from the cities. They know what will one day happen here, but they came here nonetheless. They've made their peace with it, and have, in a way, built it into their lives."

"A trade-off for living here?"

"Yes, but also, possibly, a means of control. I said earlier that a handful of us would make it to the mainland. This is true, and it is the escape plan, but what would wait for us across the channel? When the seismic event happens, there will be earthquakes, not just wave action, earthquakes that will crumble the coastal cities like they are made of sand. All along the Pacific, down to the meridian, there will be extensive damage. And nowhere more concentrated than here. If one wanted to flee that, one could head deep inland or, better, to the opposite side of the continent. But as long as one lives here, on this coast, differences in the scale of hundred of kilometres are irrelevant. When the wave hits, it will hit. The earthquake, to knock everything loose, and the wave, to wash everything clean."

"Jesus. But I had read that it will be better on the mainland, that the islands would be a kind of buffer?"

"Wishful thinking. Yes, the island chain will catch the water, divert it into many smaller channels, sieve it through the gaps between landforms, but the threat to the coastal cities has more to do with water levels than actual percussive impact. Even if the tsunami is dispersed before it comes to the coast, this would still be an immense mass of water, flooding in at a biblical scale. These are delta cities, floodplain cities, urban centres built on land that has been dredged and filled. The flood would reverse that. Let us say that the water level increases by five metres. A conservative estimate. Most of these cities are at sea level, some are, even, below it. Now, they are twenty feet below the waterline."

"I don't know if I want to know all of this."

"If you're here, you should know."

"Raising water levels. Wouldn't it just be, like, things get wet, property gets damaged, and so on?"

"It's not so much how much it rises as how it rises. Imagine a quantity of water six metres high, moving in laterally from the coast. Not so much a wave, like in the movies, but instead a sheet, a block. Do not underestimate the weight of water. You bathe in the tub in four hundred pounds of water. A cubic meter of seawater, a small amount, the volume of, say, a refrigerator box—nearly a thousand kilograms. Multiply that volume by four or five, and make it an unbroken bar for hundreds of kilometres. And all of that weight coming in at thirty, forty kilometres an hour, with even more speed close to the shore: a wall of hundreds upon hundreds of tonnes of water, advancing and crushing everything beneath it. Sweeping away bridges, houses, trees, cars, people; pulling these things into itself and pulverizing them as it continues inland."

"I definitely do not want to know this."

"I am sorry. But one should know, especially here."

"What are the odds that it will happen?"

"Do you mean, happen right now?"

"Yes, right now. While we're here."

"It is possible. It is hard to speak to time at this scale. It is three hundred years overdue, but we cannot know when it will decide to make up for its absence—it could be right now, it could be in two centuries. We believe that there is a seven percent chance it will happen within the next thirty years, but that period of time, that probability, includes this very moment. While we sit here and talk, it could be happening."

"But it isn't."

"Not yet. Or we would see it on the monitors."

"And if we do see it?"

"If we see it, we have half an hour."

"How do people stand it, knowing that at any minute this could happen and there's nothing they could do?"

"But this is how we all live, isn't it? Or it is how we should, in a way. People have died in smaller waves than this. On Peliatos, many have."

"Surfing accidents? Are they that common?"

"Common enough. Everyone on Peliatos know some-one who has died in the water. Some, the unlucky, know more than one."

Something in the set of Lena's features now makes Win want to change the subject, but just then there's some action on screen. They both turn to watch the numbers come in, and the graphs rise and fall. It's almost beautiful, if it didn't mean what it did.

CHAPTER ELEVEN

ANA RISES OUT OF THE BATH TOO QUICKLY, careless, and the pain that bursts up the cords of her neck feels nearly as bad as it was in the beginning. She lets out a little grunt of pain and comes back down into the water with a splash. She lies there, knees bent above the waterline, ears just beneath, and stares at the speckled tiles for a minute. There's no sound from the other room. When the pain fades, she tries again, more carefully this time, using the sloped back of the tub, pushing herself up against it, the skin of her back sticking and unsticking on the wet acrylic. Then she's upright, knees pulled close, and all she has to do is stand up.

She puts the brace back on before drying off even though it severely limits her reach, makes her fumble with the towel, because the pain made her worry. She doesn't know the calculus of healing but she is determined to do nothing to set herself back, to avoid prolonging this thing any more than it has to be. She's not meant to start stretching until the pain is gone. She gets dressed and it takes a long time, and in the mirror she feels pathetic, geriatric, and embarrassed even though she's alone. The wet spots she's missed with the towel cling to her clothing, cold in the unheated room, so she goes out to where the fireplace is. The television is on but Win isn't there. She sits by the fire. The waves outside are barely perceptible, the water a dark blue under the sky's darker blue, but she can still hear them, the waves.

That people would choose this, this life, she can't understand, even when she tries. Why not just visit? Why stake out a spot at the end of culture, the end of the world, and not return? Lena explained it to them, told them why people, new people, were coming to the island. They had a sense of it, Win and Ana, because that kind of person— wealthy, curious, ahead of the curve—were their clients, or at least were the clients of their employer. When Ana drove the van along the wooded highway, just as when she was in the vacant grid, she knew who the pictures were for. But she couldn't square the client with the product. Ana had no grievance with the hippies, the surfers, the recluses, hermits. She had no feelings either way; they were a category of person, like there were categories of plants or birds. She liked their host, Lena, respected her for what she had done and the fact that she had made a choice as definite and unretractable as this. She could feel why Lena would want to live so close to her work. Why the technocratic elite, burst into the stratosphere of choice and wealth, would congregate to Peliatos, was beyond her capacity to understand. It wasn't a flock yet, at least not until the flames were fanned by developers, but it would be soon. But why? Ana decides to go for a walk, grabbing a jacket, Lena's, off of the couch, stepping into her shoes, and leaving through the front door.

The van is in the trees, quiet now. The keys are in Lena's pocket from before. Ana pulls the door open, lifts herself onto the sloping seat. The blood on the air bag is brown and she folds it up and stuffs it back into the compartment in the centre of the wheel. Leaves coat the windshield, and the whole cabin is at a nauseating slant that pushes her hard against the side of the seat. Ana turns the keys in the ignition and the van, canted in the shattered mass of trees, comes shuddering back to life.

PART TWO: FIFTEEN FEET

CHAPTER ONE

MAYBE THEY'D NEVER SEEN A HELICOPTER, or maybe just they had never seen a helicopter land. He figured most people coming to the island drove or took the ferry or maybe a few sprang for the float plane, but certainly no choppers, at least not yet. So when it landed, the blades pounding and sand flying off the beach, a small crowd gathered. A reception but not really. They hung around while the chopper powered down, and after he got out they all left either because they recognized him or because they didn't recognize him. It's hard to tell with these people—not sure how fully they're off the grid. Out of the market at least, which he had a feeling around here went as the same thing. The helicopter taking off fifteen or twenty feet behind him pebbled his back with sand, left little bits in his clothes for him to find later. There wasn't a car waiting but he was close enough;

he walked down the beach to the craggy mass of rock that soon would hold the structure. There was a small cabin there that came with the lot. Who knows who lived in it or when. Before his guys got in there and redid it, below all that perfectly rectilinear gypsumboard, it was he heard some kind of fisherman's shed or surfer's squat. It didn't even have a toilet. The crew added one and a walk-in shower next to it, all glass and poured concrete. Glass and concrete and semi-gloss white—a little study in materials for him to try out as they built the real thing around him.

Kitt liked it so far. The consistency, the same trinity of materials he'd done all of his showrooms in. He was twenty years and several income brackets out from using a word like "vibes," but that's what it really was: the vibes. The room-feel. He was lying on the couch and staring up at the concrete base of the lofted bed fifteen feet up where the half-attic used to be. They knocked out the wooden stairs or what was left of them and redid them in cantilevered steel with a dangerous edge. Like a blueprint of a staircase. The skeleton of a staircase. They'd have done the same for the steps up the rock face if blasting wasn't so costly, time-wise. That was the only cost that really touched him at this point: time. A good place to be.

The shower worked. He kicked out of his pants and pulled of his shirt, both done in a material that wasn't cotton but just looked like cotton, was actually a copyrighted mix of polymers and superfine wool. A fabric with its own legal team. One-third wetsuit, water-wicking, but the point was more how it draped, how little light it reflected: the contours of the pile of cloth on the floor were hardly visible but for the sand. The sand was like dots on a motion capture suit. A slight mineral edge to the shower—that trace of sediment and salt the filtration system couldn't scrub out. The taste a memory. Despite his branding and his past, he hadn't been in salt water for three years. The well punched into the rock seventy feet before it hit the water table, but the water it pulled up was still more or less opaque. He'd have to get a second filter put in or have his water brought in from somewhere else. For that he'd need a tank the size of this cabin, sunk into the foundations. Not a problem; he could do that, could have that done. Next to the scale of the project —building a ten-thousand-square-foot structure, a third of which would be suspended out over the water and made of wafer-thin concrete with a network of rebar and counter-balanced I-beams keeping the whole thing from tipping into the ocean—a water tank would be no problem. Plus he liked the idea of having his own water and not having to rely on the island's supply. Not even rainwater, though consistent enough at these latitudes, no. Have your own. You can't depend on anything. Who knows what will happen.

Outside the cabin the first measurements had been taken and a rough blueprint was spray-painted onto rock and soil in Day-Glo orange. Kitt paced the perimeter, scuffing the fresh blast-rubber soles of his boots on the grooved rock. His fortress. In four months, three if the local council doesn't screw him over, this will all be tempered glass and poured concrete. Glass, that better sand; concrete, that better rock. Tomorrow the first crew came and it would start. He knew the invoice by memory. Huge diggers with carbide drills to perforate the stone floor and pneumatic ones to knock out chunks. An old-fashioned excavator. Subtractive work, loud and messy. He'd find out how good the soundproofing of his cabin really was. He walked through what would be the living room to the edge of the cliff. If he jumped, would he make it? Maybe not with the boots. No risk of hitting rock, though, with the face cutting back towards the house underneath him. No risk of hitting bottom, either—even at low tide the ocean at the base of the cliff was thirty feet. Measurements he learned when he was considering driving piles into the seabed, before the idea of levering the whole thing out into thin air and balanced right on the edge. He liked that image and liked not having to worry about underwater digging, about underwater fauna tests, about insurance for underwater contractors. He looked way out over the edge; the water was the same colour as the stone and was chopped up into foam here and there by the waves. Out past the drop-off the Pacific was nothing for thousands of miles and it was perfect.

THE FIRST THING TO GO WAS COLOUR. THAT'S WHEN it changed, went from being what you wore every day to the beach to what you wore once or twice a month. The logic flipped: from high visibility to low. He sold off the warning orange and supermarine by the crate to a fabric dealer in Marin County, two thousand square yards in total, and took the cash and invested it in a postage stamp of *habutai* imported from a source so well kept that he had to buy someone a crate of wine just to get the address. That was the start of it, or at least the start of it getting started. Dress code at the store level went from being non-existent to exacting. Boxes of uniforms arrived on the same day at every shop across the country, one-piece garments in a grey only a shade or two off of black, fabric that hung so geometrically and with so few zones of tension and overlap that the floor crews, those that stayed, didn't even have to be told not to personalize them. He thought first of cutting out the music entirely then instead commissioned a post-rock group he liked to write a twelve-hour long composition that would play during store hours, seamlessly on a loop. There were no mandates on dress in the office but people took the hint. He'd been surrounding himself with outsiders anyway—non-surfers, people not from coastal towns but from port cities. He put everything, even things released two months ago, on clearance. He changed his mind and had it black-bagged instead and tossed in the back of storage. The stores sat empty for two weeks looking like minimalist sculpture; he kept them open. It worked. When the first line was released, a ten-item unisex fall series, the shops filled and emptied within two hours of opening and the customers took everything with them that wasn't bolted down. He made more money that day than they had the entire quarter, and it wasn't just because the new stuff was priced four or five times higher than the old: he had hit some cultural nerve, some sweet spot, and perfected a style before it even existed.

That night at the production building Kitt threw a massive party and, coked out of his mind, dragged out all of the garbage bags full of yesterday's product and piled them up in the centre of the warehouse and set them on fire.

All the rolls of fabric stacked in the stockroom were an unwavering monochrome from then on, but underneath the dye the material was evolving—changing from the dealer-bought chambray and dense-weave cotton to something interpenetrated with strands of what could only be described as technology. His orders dovetailed between suppliers several worlds apart. In the same day he'd place an order for high-strain-resistant neoprene from a deep-sea diving company in Martigues, and another for thousand-thread chiffon from Padua that would disintegrate in the rain between cab and front door. He cross-wove clear polymers into vicuña wool. He mixed materials spun by the salivary glands of worms with those produced by scientists under non-compete clauses. He was looking for a kind of stealth, a material that would be so unlike any other cloth that it would hardly register as fabric at all.

When someone drove a truck into his main downtown storefront he replaced the windows, pushed the heap of mangled shelves and displays to one side, and moved a splinter unit of manufacturing into the remaining space. They worked, machines whirring, separated from the street by a thin layer of floor-to-ceiling plate glass. He never got around to shipping out the wreckage—he couldn't resist how it looked, divided off from the dozen workstations by a row of mannequins, the sharp metal folds like the discarded skin of some new and hungry animal.

CHAPTER TWO

THE DIGGERS ARRIVE, AND THE CONCUSSION of the drills all firing in unison is enough to make the black corrugated steel walls of his cabin rattle from thirty feet away. He watches as the machinery carves out a negative image of the structure into the rock. He circles around the construction site for an hour or so, and the progress is too slow to hold his interest, so he goes back inside to kill some time on the internet. But the whole shed is shaking at a high frequency, like a tuning fork, so after checking his email and grabbing his things he gets out of there. He's got wheels now, a black Mercedes G-Class from the eighties, which he likes because he read somewhere that they were designed to be heli-dropped into the jungle and assembled by hand. His came on the ferry, and pre-assembled, but he likes the narrative anyway. A week before he had it brought over he had the interior reupholstered

with a roll of his new fabric, making sure that the uphol-
sterers gave him all of the leftover scraps so that he could
dispose of them himself. In the low light under the tree-
cover, the interior of the wagon is so consistently, abso-
lutely black that the windows look tinted. A Kitt Feldt special edition, of one.

He pulls into the parking lot of the resort, some upper-
middle-class paradise with alright food where he's been
eating three meals a day instead of using the hot plate in
his cabin. It was cheaper in the end to book a room at the
highest tier, the level that includes complimentary meals
at the restaurant, with the added bonus of twenty-four-
hour gym access. He crosses the lobby and hits the key fob
against the elevator panel, goes up one floor to the gym.
After he's done a circuit he fobs back into the elevator,
rides it to the top floor, and has a shower in his untouched
room. He notes that his view at home is better than the one
out of the suite's window.

The takeout container on the passenger seat is as
over-designed as the hotel, made from a type of recycled
cardboard that looks more exclusive than non-recycled
cardboard would. He's steering carefully but is pretty
sure that, due to the neglected road, the shaved beef and
white truffle carpaccio will arrive looking like dog food.
He gets back just in time: they're finishing up the drilling
and gouging. After the machines clear out he descends a
ladder down into the foundations of his home. He skirts
around the edge of the square pit dug way down into
the rock that will hold his twenty-cubic-foot water tank.
This whole basement, minus the tank and boiler and the

filter-pump unit and the geothermal heat exchanger, will be storage. Except for the shelter, which won't be in the basement proper but instead in the back of the foundation, underneath the bedroom, accessible by a stairwell he's put behind one of the closet doors. He climbs back up to ground level and retrieves the box of leftovers. He gives the excavation a final look over. The building is already impressive, and it's just a hole.

On the way to his cabin, he's intercepted by his crew's structural engineer with some final details about the pouring of the foundation, which will happen tomorrow, and a set of modifications he approves because he trusts him with the automatic trust that the overspecialized have for one another. Kitt is forty-two and done learning, has learned everything he needed to master to make a little surf wear company out of two sewing machines and a closet and then turn it into a multi-billion-dollar brand. Let other people do the learning for him now.

That evening he eats the leftovers cold from the fridge with a six-pack of beer and watches a movie with subtitles and passes out on the couch. When he wakes up it's dawn, the skylight a uniform Pantone grey. He puts his jacket on and steps outside, the air full of mist, or rain, and hears nothing but the dull crash of the surf. And then he hears conversation, voices, muffled, coming from somewhere near him. He holds onto the open door of the cabin, feeling all of the built-up heat exit around him. The neighbouring lot is a hundred, two hundred feet away, the road way behind. Another pause. The sound starts up again, low, lower than the waves or the wind moving the tops of the trees around, but it's there. He shuts the door quietly and heads in the direction of the voices, towards, he realizes, the pit. There's too much cloud cover for moonlight to get through and the rock and dirt and moss are all uniformly black underfoot. He should be hungover but the adrenaline works better than the electrolyte supplement he forgot to take last night. He feels completely aware, completely present. He's stepping deliberately, quietly, careful not to alert them, whoever they are, before he sees them. Before he's able to figure out what to do. He's hoping it's as dark as it feels and that he's hidden even out past the tree cover. The fabric should help with that. But it's not total dark: there's light coming from inside the pit, the foundations. It looks a lot like but couldn't possibly be a campfire. A campfire, in his foundations.

Kitt stands on the edge of the excavation for a few minutes before he catches their attention. He sees them, lit up at the back end of the pit where the wind wouldn't come in. There's six or seven of them, their bodies leaning together towards the warmth. In the firelight he can see their faces. He knows them. Not personally, but he knows their life, their type. They probably came here on a trip five or ten years ago to check out some wave. And stayed, getting whatever job they could whenever they could. He knew losers like these from back when he shared a hobby with them, lifers, all riding the same wave worse and worse as their knees gave out and their reflexes were shot by ventilating their brains with drinking and smoking cheap weed. And then after some point the jobs were all gone, but they stayed. And what for? Rooming up with friends paying smaller and smaller fractions of rent to share a bed-room, a bed, a closet. Until even that fell through. Thirty-somethings who spent the year bouncing between two campsites, packing up their stuff every time they hit the fourteen-day limit.

Finally someone in the group looks up and notices him. Kitt shouts down into the pit: "Get the fuck out."

"What?" That sleepy, chiller-than-thou voice. They all stand and look up at him.

"Get, the fuck, out. Get off my property. You're tres-passing."

"We've been coming here for years, man. Who are you?"

"I'm the guy who owns this construction site and the land it's on, and you're going to leave. Are you seriously having a fire in my house?"

"It's not a house, man." The same one talking the whole time. Their leader, or the only one not too messed up to speak?

"Shut up. Get out. I'll give you five minutes to put that out, pick up your stuff, and leave."

"What, are you using it?" The nerve of this wastoid. Does he realize how much shit he's in?

"'Using it.' My foundations? Using my construction site? I'm calling the cops." Kitt steps back from the edge and pulls out his phone, which, for once, has a signal.

"They won't get here until the morning."

"What?"

"The cops. The pigs, man. Even if you call them there's only one and the station's the next island over."

He puts his phone away. They're probably right. This fucking place. God forbid something urgent would ever happen here. Who else could he call? His crew is all on the mainland, and he knows nobody else here except for the chef at the hotel. He's not going to be able to personally drag this group of shitheads off of his property by himself.

Then he has a better idea. Why should they leave, after all?

The ladder felt sturdy on his way down this morning, so he's surprised at how light it is. It must be some kind of high-end reinforced aluminum, strong but featherweight. That's good. He likes that. This lets him lift it easily, standing with his toes against the edge, with hardly any effort. He's already got the ladder halfway up the wall before the kids realize what's happening and by that time it's out of their reach anyway, even when they jump for it. He slows down, then, and does the rest leisurely, walking his hands up rung by rung, laughing, dipping it down from time to time and jerking it back up when they go for it. One kid keeps trying to leap up and grab it but his outstretched hand is nowhere close. Kitt lays the ladder down a few paces from the excavation and then walks back to the edge. The deadbeats are all freaking out now, screaming and yelling, especially when he walks over to their side of the pit and starts kicking gravel down onto them. If he could, he'd piss out their fire. He hates them, their righteous laziness, their lack of initiative, hates them for how square, how stuck-up, they make him feel in moments like this, when he's more of a revolutionary than any of them can imagine. They've put their whole lives into a dead culture, going nowhere, and it sickens him and fills him with embarrassment and rage. He hates them for reminding him of an entire set of people he's put so much effort into avoiding, for contaminating every good spot left on the whole long coast. And he hates, hates, their shitty clothing. The gravel pings off the sheets of plywood, off the concrete, off the back of empty surfer heads. A few minutes more and he gets tired of it, so he decides to head back to bed.

On the way back towards the cabin, that's when something really beautiful happens: it starts to rain.

CHAPTER THREE

KITT WAKES UP FOR THE SECOND TIME TO A massive rumbling coming through the walls of the cabin: the diggers in motion. He leaps out of bed and out the door and sees that the concrete pourers are here, and his whole crew is, and he's in his underwear. His civil engineer is standing not far off from the cabin and when he sees Kitt he walks over.

"Wild night last night?" He points to a clear plastic bag full of empties that someone's collected from the pit and left by the scrap heap.

"Huh. No, had some squatters in the hole."

"Figures. Goddamn deadbeats on this island. Did you call the cops?"

"Nah, what's the point. They were just kids. Thanks for getting them out of there, though."

"What do you mean? There was no one here when I came in."

"Even better."

Huh. They must have gotten on each other's shoulders, or maybe one of them thought to use his phone and call someone. Whatever, it's not like he really had a plan for what to do with them. He's glad to have made them miserable, at least for a time, and he's glad he didn't have to handle the cleanup.

Kitt jogs over to the excavation, which—it must be later in the day than he thought, because it's completely transformed."The moulds for the concrete are finished, and with the wooden framework in place the structure pops into focus like a wire-frame rendering. He can see where the slabs will be that hold his water tank, can see the additional heft the concrete will take on the ocean-facing side to support the weight of the cantilevered living room. The walls of the shelter are marked out and the rebar's sticking out from the wooden enclosures like raw spaghetti. He walks around to the far side and sees that they've already poured two of the four massive blocks at each edge of the foundation, ten-by-ten-by-twenty feet of solid concrete sunk deep into the ground. Last night these were just pits in the rock. Now, made pure vertical bulk, the columns are, he'll even say, *triumphant.*

He showers and spends the rest of the workday popping out once in a while to check on the progress, then going back to researching for next year's line. It gets dark quickly, the short northern day shortened by his waking up halfway through it. Soon there's not enough light for the work to continue and someone comes by to knock on his door and tell him they're packing up. He heads outside for one last look over, the construction site lit up piecemeal by white-hot halogen lights, and he's happy. The work is going quickly, the town council hasn't raised shit with him yet, and soon the walls will be up and he will be able to walk through something that six months ago was just a sketch, a dream. His best work. The cliché, but it's true. He has the feeling that his whole life, all of those wasted years making t-shirts and rash guards, has been leading up to this, has been validated by this—the house, the new designs, the *real* stuff.

He's been back in the cabin for an hour or so and is starting to think about dinner when there's a second knock on his door. Thinking it's his civil engineer or someone else from his crew running something by him last minute he hops up, book in hand, and opens the door. It's not. Under the cabin's overhang is a kid wearing a paint-spattered hoodie under a denim jacket. He's leaning from foot to foot, with the cold or nerves or who knows what else, and when Kitt opens his mouth to speak the kid interjects.

"You fucking monster."

Kitt doesn't know how to respond to this. He recognizes the voice from last night.

"What?"

"Where's my sister?" The kid spits the words out, leaning way forward, his body all threat.

"Sister? What are you talking about? Calm down." This kid looks terrible. Like he'd been up all night, or like he'd sleeping outside for months. His eyes are yellow, and so is his skin, yellow and waxy like a corpse. Or maybe it's just the light. He looks like a fucking demon. Kitt backs up a bit to get some space in between them and this must look like he's going to slam the door because the kid jumps forward to close the gap. Now he's right up in Kitt's face.

"What, did you do, to my fucking sister?"

"What is this? What are you saying I did? Take it easy, man."

"We were here last night. Remember? Your asshole trick with the ladder?"

"Yeah, well, I asked you to leave."

"We did. We got out, we called a guy, he got us out."

"Good for you. You know I can still call the cops, right?"

"Shut up. You don't know what's going on. You're in big fucking trouble, man." The kid's voice is hysterical, unsteady, almost, it seemed to Kitt, in tears. He didn't have time for this shit. He made a mental note to book some security next week. He clearly needed to establish a perimeter.

"You have five minutes before I call —"

"Then listen. Okay? You need to listen. Where is she? Did you see anyone on the lot?"

"Aside from you assholes? No."

"No one at all? Are you sure?" The voice was pleading, not angry. Kitt wasn't sure what this kid wanted to hear.

"No, just my crew. And me. What the fuck is going on?"

"We got out last night. With your ladder. Your fucking ladder. And we're back in town when I realize, where is she? She wasn't with us. We went out looking for her, all of us, all night. Couldn't find her. Phone's dead. We figured she wandered off on the walk back so we get flashlights, we comb the whole area. A few hours of this and we call some more people, we try her friends' places. It's not till morning when I realize: she wasn't with us by the fire, she was by herself. She was asleep already, she had taken her sleeping bag down into one of those *holes*."

"No. No she wasn't."

"I run back and it's morning and your crew's already there, and I don't want trouble, so I wait down the street. I figure they haven't found her yet. Then this big cement truck pulls out onto the road and drives off. Then I got this bad feeling, I had to see, so I came up back through the trees and there it was. You'd already done it and there was nothing I could do."

"I'd done what."

"You—you filled up the hole. You buried her in concrete."

"No. That's insane. There's just no fucking way."

"Yes you did." He's close, now, right up in Kitt's face. "You *killed my sister,* man, you *buried her alive.*"

WHEN KITT IS SURE THAT THE KID HAS LEFT HE BOLTS out of the cabin and grabs the ladder, swinging it overhead and into the pit. He comes down it fast, two rungs at a time, and when he's down into the foundation he runs, hopping over woodwork, to the two blocks of concrete. He crouches down to where they meet the rock and down there he realizes: he's being fucked with. There's no way.

He's being fucked with. *Oh, goddamn, shit, the ladder.* He gets up and runs towards it, his lungs totally empty, and catches his ankle on exposed rebar but doesn't feel it. He's an idiot, falling for this. The rest of them were waiting in the woods, waiting for him to go down into the hole. He left his phone in the cabin and the door unlocked. It's fucking cold out and they were going to fuck him, to leave him in here. Mess with, steal, trash his stuff. His laptop was full, fucking full, of sensitive shit. Everything for next year. All his banking shit. He's been played, *Jesus fuck.* And he fell right into their trap.

The ladder is still there and he grabs onto it, leaning onto it with all his weight so they can't pull it up. He waits, but nothing happens. The lot is quiet. Nobody is there.

CHAPTER FOUR

ANA IS ASLEEP IN THE NARROW BED IN LENA'S guest room, Win in a matching one across from her. She has kicked the covers back and is lying on the mattress on her side, her back towards the wall, her knees curled up towards her chest.

In a dream, she rises like a weather balloon, up to the ceiling, the roof opening up to let her through, and into the night. The house drops away, is the size of a van, then a matchbox, then a flake of shingle, and she keeps rising, riding on thermals like a seabird. The wind changes, and the mattress drifts inland, away from the shore. Below her is the whole island, like melted dark-green wax puckered up in the middle to its flattened ridge. It is night, but she is not cold, even with all of the wind.

And then a sound, like the groan of a leviathan, vibrates everything around her.

There's something in the water, a huge, glossy fold, a black wall as wide as the horizon, and it's doubling, tripling, growing with a terrible, exponential logic, accompanied by that horrifying groan, until it has blocked out the sky. It draws forward to meet her, its colossal jet-black curve of water rolling over the island, and pauses, inches from her pillow. It's quiet now. The wind has stopped, and the groan has turned into a low, motor-like hum.

The black shape hangs there, lapping at the edges of the trailing bedsheet, and then in a rush folds over her and swallows her whole.

CHAPTER FIVE

THE NEXT DAY NO ONE SHOWS UP TO THE construction site. Kitt checks his calendar, scans through his emails—yes, they're supposed to be there, work was scheduled; they were going to pour the rest of the foundation. He checks the ferry schedule to see if this is some kind of regional holiday, to see if service is reduced or suspended or if there was an accident. But it's business as usual. It's eleven o'clock when Kitt calls the lead contractor and is told that his crew is on the island but they've been stopped at the ferry terminal by the police.

Kitt has a lawyer on retainer, corporate law, but he's used him on some matters that push the definition of corporate. He calls him and explains the situation. He's confident that this is a lot of smoke, that once the cops talk to him they'll realize it's all bullshit. His lawyer concurs. Kitt asks about best courses of action, how to get this thing over with as quickly as possible, and the lawyer is going through the steps with him when the regional sheriff knocks on his cabin door.

Even the official uniform on this island feels twee, would be camp if it was in any way self-aware. He's dressed in green, with a hat that Kitt can't believe—he looks like a park ranger, like a Boy Scout leader. Kitt knew he'd have to work hard to take this all seriously, but not *this* hard. The sheriff, after some friendly opening banter, apologizes to Kitt for him not being told in a more straightforward manner; he was on the same ferry as the construction crew, and it just made more sense to detain—*detain!*—them then and there and tell Kitt afterwards. The sheriff says he's not sure but if there was going to be an investigation it would likely be against Kitt's crew of contractors and workers, and not him. He was, after all, just their customer. Kitt doesn't tell him that this isn't true—that he hired them on as employees, even made a special subsidiary of his company to manage the construction and make cash flow and structures of power easier, to give him complete oversight and ultimate responsibility over the project. Technically speaking Kitt is the foreman, but he doesn't tell this to the sheriff. He's happy playing the maligned innocent, because at bottom that is, in this scenario, what he is. Kitt just tells him about the events of the past two days—leaving out the ladder and the kicking of rocks, at the suggestion of his lawyer—and hopes that this will be enough.

When the sheriff tells him that, with even the slightest suspicion of foul play, construction will have to be halted until an investigation is undertaken, Kitt clenches his teeth and nods like a person who understands. But when he learns that given the nature of the accusation, federal police must be brought in—and, given the remoteness of the location, this might take a few weeks—and that federal police will want a thorough questioning of the construction crew, the group of youths, and their families—Kitt loses his composure and does something that probably damages his case, if there was a case, if he thought that there was the slightest chance that any of this shit was real and not just loony islander bullshit, and the sheriff leaves in a huff.

Kitt grabs his phone and dials his lawyer. The call connects to laughter on the other end. After a pause, the lawyer tells him he shouldn't worry. He'd gotten the name of Kitt's accuser from the local police station and done some digging in the records. Marcus Farwell was juvie trash, a past offender with a number of petty charges who had been in and out of trouble with the cops since he was a teenager on the other side of the continent. Of course he'd end up on a small island somewhere, every bridge having been burnt. Everything about this situation screamed delinquency: trespassing, attempted squatting, slander, false accusations. He couldn't lay a finger on Kitt, legally speaking. If anything, with his record, this could land him back in prison—real jail, this time, since Farwell was now twenty-nine. Kitt is shocked at this detail; the kid looked a decade younger. He looked like shit, but he looked like a teenager. Was he sure?

"Well, you know, eternal youth," his lawyer says. "Whatever. What you want to do, first thing, is have a meeting with the small-town cops and the town council. Tell them that you want to help the investigation as best you can. Get them on your side, show them that there's a criminal in their midst. These kinds of people love a good witch hunt. They'll probably burn him at the stake as a purification rite for the island, or maybe just put him on an ice floe and kick."

"Ha-ha."

"I'm probably not that far off the mark. Do you know anything about the kinds of communities that crop up here? They're a self-contained system, aside from the Feds, that is. They'll want to settle it their own way. Once they see that you're the victim here, the victim of attempted abuse of law, the case will be over by the time the real cops even get there. I'm willing to bet they'll even let you keep working until they show up. That is, of course, if you promise not to use any more of their townspeople for building materials."

So this is what Kitt does. The sheriff left him the contact info for the police station and told him to call by no later than the end of the day. Well, he's calling right now. He's surprised at how readily the sheriff's office agrees to the meeting—small-town values, he supposes—and is pleased that they offer to contact the town council on his behalf. It's a good thing that he has an in-between; he's already pushed his luck with the council enough, having spent a month of back-and-forth with them muscling past property lines and finding shortcuts through the maze of building regulations. Still, Kitt is sure this will all be set aside once they've heard him out.

It's Friday; the meeting is set for Monday. Kitt has the weekend to relax, to shake off some of this madness, to get ready to be his most winning self for his little audience. To get as much material on this Marcus Farwell as he can. He wonders if the resort is still serving brunch.

CHAPTER SIX

THE MAN ON TOP OF KITT IS HEAVY, MAYBE two hundred pounds, and his forearm is pushed hard against the base of Kitt's skull. He cries out in pain and tries to keep his face from being crushed into the ground. He's being held tight, a knee in his lower back, pinned on his stomach. The man leans back into his knee and Kitt's vision swims. The man pushes even harder and he feels like he is going to vomit, is sure he's going to. He's covered in sweat and making sounds of a low, automatic nature. The arm against the back of his head pulls back, the man's weight shifts, and before Kitt can wriggle free the hand grips his hair, pulling his head back, the muscles at the front of his neck tearing, until he is looking into the man's eyes, upside-down. The man has a smile on his face.

"Let me know if this is too hard."

"Too hard," Kitt gasps. His head is released and the

weight is taken off of his back. The man kneels beside him and rubs at his shoulders and legs firmly enough to push him flat.

"You're off this week. Unresponsive. You need to keep working at this, or else all of our progress will be lost. Have you been doing the exercises?"

"I'm trying to. I'm busy."

"Never be too busy for your body." The man stands, straightens his gi, and extends a hand. Kitt takes it and lets himself be pulled upright.

After they've vaporized some weed and done some stretches, Kitt sends the man away and turns on the shower. He looks at himself in the mirror, fingers the welts around his shoulders. Everything hurts, which is the point. You have to subtract before you can add. Kitt had found the one qi gong practitioner in the city who referred to ligaments and musculature instead of chi, and then paid him to come over on the ferry once a week. That he had access to medical-grade marijuana was an added benefit. This was the one thing Kitt would allow himself; he had put a body of water between himself and his old dealer, who mostly sold synthetics, the really good and really bad stuff, and this was partially on purpose, was part of the point of coming here and building this fortress. The rest was a vague sense of crisis. A feeling of foreboding, a need to burrow and hole up. Kitt watched the news like everyone else, after all. The hermetically sealed bathroom—another test run, another material study—fills with steam, and the mirror clouds over.

After his shower Kitt gets dressed and walks to the

edge of his property. The stairs his crew carved out of the rock lead down towards sea level before splitting off to the beach on one side and, on the other, to a small cave, water-worn, a divot in the cliff face cut out by millennia of wave action. He's not sure what to do with this space, but he owns it, and will find something to do with it soon enough. He at first had the idea of connecting it to the house with a tunnel but when he shared his plans the civil engineer made evasive comments. Drilling through that much rock, and horizontally, not from the top-down, would require the kind of machine they used to bore subway tunnels. Simply extending the exterior staircase down to it made more sense. Sure, fine. As he rounds the corner he sees, perched along the bottom ledge of the cave, a row of empties. Oh, *fuck off*, he thinks, and the kicks them one by one into the ocean, far out, where the grey waves swallow them up.

The wind is bringing in some action—ten, fifteen-foot breakers. Kitt remembers this spot, or a spot like it, the consistent break that brought him here back when he cared. The same wave over and over again like it was playing on loop.

It was almost two decades ago that Kitt had driven out to Peliatos for the first time. He had heard rumours and wanted to see for himself. He was alone, alone on the early ferry, alone on the beach, the pre-social-media paradise of unbroadcasted surf. He took his wetsuit out of the Rubbermaid in the back of his car, tossed it on the hood, and stripped down to his underwear. It was cold, fucking cold, in and out of the water, and he had hoped that'd keep people away—this was nothing like the room-temperature ocean further south. There was hardly enough sun to light up the breaks. He tugged his wetsuit on, the stupid one-legged hop, unclipped his board from the roof rack, and jogged towards the looping, restarting wave.

The very last time he came out, he had to park his car way down the dirt road and walk. It was an Infiniti then, the car, in line with all of the beat-up station wagons and five-door hatchbacks. He didn't come back again after that. Partly because how blown out it was getting, how annoying it was to wait in line for the ferry, and then in line for a wave, but mostly because he didn't have the time. His company had just gone public.

Kitt sat down in the cave, and looked out. There's no one on the water today, at least not here. It probably had something to do with the rocky outcroppings that framed this chunk of water, instant death if you came off wrong. It was a hostile beach, abandoned by the locals. The helicopter landing was probably the most traffic this cove had ever seen. This was good: he didn't want to look out of the glass wall of his living room and see surfers. Or have them see him.

THE TOWN HALL WAS MORE LIKE A LODGE. THOUGH all of the buildings on the island were, all tended towards some kind of rustic kitsch, even the new ones. All of the buildings but the resort, and Kitt's, when it was finished. He was sure there would be more soon. More structures that didn't work the cliché of the house-in-the-woods. Buildings that mirrored the landscape instead of satirizing it. His plans, his home, truly fit in, and not by aping the narrative of the settlers, or pioneers, or whatever. He was building his hearth from chunks of rock blasted from the island. The concrete was imported, sure, but it was the same all-over grey of the landscape, not cartoonish cedar shingle and forest-green trim. Kitt looked forward to the day when the whole island was buildings like his, homes and stores and restaurants squatting low and unobtrusive in the landscape instead of sticking out in a cheesy Disneyland of rough-hewn beams and wood-burnt signage. Kitt knew the locals would hate it at first, but they'd get used to it. They'd learn to like it. It would bring variety, blessed variety, to an island full of the same kind of house, the same kind of shop, the same kind of art, the same kind of person. The door had been shut on this island for decades, until only a certain kind of mindset existed there—closed-off, vaguely liberal, suspicious of the whole continent at its back. This would change. And maybe then there'd be more than one place to eat that wasn't a granola-slinging dive. If there wasn't, he'd have to open one. Not a bad idea. He had friends who would lend a hand.

He clicks the lock on the G-Wagon and crosses the gravel lot to the front of the building. The tacked-up postings spill out over the corkboard and onto the wooden siding, pinned and stapled wherever there is space. Kitt stops and reads. *FOR RENT: one br in large home. looking for good roommate, clean, loves the outdoors. no drugs. $400. ask raldo at the spindrifter ecolodge for details. available right now.* And, *Free Community Yoga Classes. Bikram* •

Vinyasa • Ashtanga • Hatha • Unaligned. Tuesday-Thursday at Electric Karma, 3419 Winnow Dr. B.Y.O.M. (Bring Your Own Mat). All Skills Welcome! They went on, and fucking on: *Looking for job. Will work kitchens, gardening, administrative, design work, office work, temping. Well-qualified. Good employee. Call 778 829 9917 for offers/leads/more info. PROTECT OUR ISLAND AGAINST THE FORCES OF EVIL. email peliatos.defenders@greenlink.com. Always accepting new members. STOLEN BIKE: if you or anyone you know sees a 2015 polyride hybrid street/trail, slate blue, all factory parts, it is STOLEN call patti @ 250-836-3820 right away. namaste.* Kitt pulls out his phone and snaps a picture of the "Defenders" posting.

A beat-up old truck pulls into the parking lot and the driver, some old-timer, gets out. When she walks up to the billboard, Kitt moves along and with his phone-hand pushes open the door to the building. As he does so he can feel the old lady's eyes on him. His clothing—more of the patented fabric, this time woven and looped and stitched into slim-cut slacks and a loose fitting crew neck—marks him, *because* it's invisible. The woman isn't head-to-toe paisley like most of them. She's in fact pretty well dressed for an islander, but where her gaberdine and birdseye linen are all earth tones and texture, his uniform is as black and void as outer space. She follows him inside. Kitt goes into the unisex washroom, locks the door, and rehearses his victim-face in the mirror. Once he's gotten used to it, he leaves and finds the conference room.

The room is small but it is packed. The woman is there, along with the sheriff Kitt met earlier, and a whole

selection of islanders. This is, he's told, the town council—government employees, teachers, shopkeepers,
parents and surfers and baristas, brought together on a
volunteer basis every month to discuss the good of the
island. It sounds creepy as hell to him. This summit is a
special meeting, but they run through the standard opening anyhow, along with a community news report that he
has to clench his teeth through to keep from laughing.
Small, small, small, these people's worlds. He wonders
when the last time an outsider sat in on one of these, and
is sure he's the first. He hopes it doesn't end in a prayer or
a massage circle.

With the preliminaries over, the room shifts to the
matter at hand. The case is outlined by the old woman,
clearly the leader of the council. Kitt's dying of boredom
while he waits for his turn, waits while she tells the room
stuff he already knows. He can hear everyone else taking
notes: night-time young adults camping run-in construction crew foundation pour concrete accusation missing
person investigation halt construction federal. Finally, it's
his turn to address the group. All eyes are on him but he
can't quite read the expressions. *Here goes.*

"I am here to help." Kitt pauses for effect. Some regional-
production shit, but he knows it will work on these
people. "It pains me that I am meeting all of you, meeting my new community, under such circumstances, but if
this is how I'm introduced, let me simply say, I am here to
help. We"—his lawyer told him to use this word as much
as physically possible—"*we* have been told that someone, a
young person, has lost their life. There must be a thorough

investigation; I am glad that we have the expertise of the law both on and off of the island to see this through. But we, too, have a role to play. I am told that someone has died on my construction site, has died, practically, in my home. I cannot do anything but extend my help to this community, to promise whatever assistance I can give to the island in determining, as soon as possible, whether this awful claim is true. If this is true, it is a tragedy, appalling, a horrific accident that can not be undone, but we can try, if we try, to heal the damage it has done to the community." He gets some assenting nods, some vocalized agreement. "If this is true. But I don't think it is."

The air leaves the room with a whoosh. The sheriff looks up.

"What?"

"I don't think that the claim brought forth is true, and I can say this because I alone, in this room, was there that night, am close enough to the situation to know it for what it really is. I see that my accuser, Mr. Farwell, isn't here today. This is a shame. I'd say I'd like to get to know him better, if I didn't already know him too well." Kitt can feel their attention, knows that it's working. "I met him only once, and not under the best circumstances. He and his friends were trespassing on my property the night of the eighth. They had broken into my construction site, thinking that it was abandoned, but it wasn't: I was there. I have a cabin on the property—small but comfortable—where I've been living while the main residence is built. They woke me up, Farwell and his friends. They had somehow gotten into the foundations of my building, and were having a party down

there. From what you know of Marcus, this shouldn't surprise you. This is, as I've learned, the kind of thing that he
does—trespassing, breaking and entering, squatting, van-
dalism, public indecency. This is the sort of thing that got
him into juvenile detention as a youth, and, well, old hab-
its die hard. That we, that a small, close-knit community
like Peliatos, would tolerate such behaviour—such criminal activity—surprises me. But I won't tolerate it. I told the
intruders to leave, figuring I could count on their sense
of decency. Maybe they thought the site was abandoned,
that they were doing no harm. But this is, I'll remind you,
an active construction site, and private property. It was a
place of work. By being there they were endangering all of
us and breaking the law. I asked them to leave my home,
but they wouldn't listen, and instead yelled abuse at me. I
won't repeat what they said, but it wasn't pretty.

"What kind of person does something like that?
Breaks into someone's property, and then when caught
shows no shame, and in fact assaults *me*, treats me like I
was in the wrong? A person like Marcus Farwell, a known
delinquent with no sense of responsibility, and no sense of
consequence. Though maybe he does understand consequence, in his own way: he knew that, to get back at me—
for what? For asking him to leave my property? To leave
me in peace?—he could do a simple thing. He could rely
on the suspicion that small communities have for new-
comers, he could rely on his ability to abuse the the law, he
could take advantage of the good faith of his neighbours.
He could accuse me of something, and then stand back
and watch the fallout.

"Maybe I shouldn't be so upset. To his credit, he and his friends did leave, at some point in the night, after they'd had their fun, after they'd made a mess of my property. He could have done worse. He has done worse things, before. He could have burnt down my cabin; he does have a predilection for arson, doesn't he? It could have happened; maybe it would have if I hadn't interrupted. But, then again, wasn't what he did even worse than that? With this accusation, he's hurt more than just me. He's injured all of us. He's spread a terrible lie that has brought pain to his community, *our* community, has made us believe that there has been a horrific death, and has wrapped me up in it as an accomplice to murder.

"There is no murder, just the reckless abuse of our trust. Does his story even seem possible? Don't you think that it's a bit unlikely that a crew of highly-trained construction workers would be working under anything but the most stringent safety protocols? Do you think that they wouldn't notice a sleeping teenage girl in their construction site, that they'd somehow build a building on top of her? Well, they didn't. There was no murder. But there was a crime, the crime of false accusations, and one with many accomplices—his sister, if he has one, who has gone along with this, his friends who were with him that night and, with him, broke into my property. And us, too—if we let him get away with what he's done."

There is a hush in the room as Kitt looks around from face to face. He's done a good job. When the ringleader, the old woman, sees that he's finished, she speaks up.

"We thank you for the comprehensiveness of your

account. Are there any comments or responses to Mr. Feldt?"

The room remains quiet—what could there be to say? They let a wolf into their midst, and now they realize it. How they hadn't realized it before now, Kitt doesn't know; surely Farwell had been doing stuff like this for years. Maybe they overlooked it out of the goodness of their kind, provincial hearts. Well, that was about to change. The leader scanned the room, and then addressed the gathering once more.

"If no one else would like to speak up, I will. With the permission of the council, of course." Everyone nodded—all these people do is fucking *nod*—and so she continued.

"What Mr. Feldt has said is compelling. He offers revelatory information about our situation. Revelatory, but, I feel, under-informed. Do not misunderstand me—I do not doubt that what he says about the night in question is true. If he was there, and saw these things, I believe him. We know, it is an uncomfortable fact, that 'squatting,' or, at least, spending a night or two in this way, has been a reality for some time among our island's youth. Many of them are not able to pay rent, have been abandoned by families, or have lost their jobs, or have fallen on hard times otherwise, and have had to resort to this. These are lean times in the world at large, and Peliatos is not immune. We have learned to accept this, to let the practice continue, even if it is unpleasant for all, because it is a lesser social ill than if we were to ban it and confront the youth of our community with an impossible situation. Perhaps we should have informed Mr. Feldt of this—agreement, if you would call it that, amongst the residents of this island.

"Does this permit these young men and women to be disrespectful to those who provide them shelter? Not at all. What Marcus and his friends have done is shameful, and Mr. Feldt is justified in his frustration. We can provide them shelter, but our obligation can, of course, only go so far. It upsets me that these young members of our community would behave in such a way, especially towards a newcomer. It upsets me to hear of their inconsiderate behaviour, but I won't deny it. I believe Mr. Feldt on this.

"What I have more difficulty in believing is his account of the following events. Not because it is not possible that a member of our community would lie to us, even to a criminal extent; we are, despite our best intentions, no better or worse than the rest of our fellow human beings. Anything is possible. What makes me doubt Mr. Feldt is that his whole sense of the situation is based on a perception of one individual, Marcus Farwell, and that this image is based entirely on the young man's past. From the supposed criminal and deviant nature of Farwell —"

"Supposed? I've seen the records. This isn't a supposition. Are you kidding me? Do all of you people really not know? The kid's a bad apple. He's done some pretty real shit in his past."

"This may well be. But that was his past, a lifetime ago. And from these remote events —"

"Remote? *Remote*. We're talking seven, eight years ago."

"I kindly ask Mr. Feldt to yield the floor; he's had his turn. Lena, you can continue."

"This is insane. I have proof. He stole a car back in 2007. He drove it into the ocean. He's robbed people. He's been caught in possession of controlled substances. How could you possibly be defending this kid?" The woman waited, patiently, for him to be done, and then went on as if he hadn't spoken.

"Mr. Feldt has extrapolated, based on one young man's troubled youth, an entire narrative of intrigue, deception, and malicious foul play. His story is tantalizing, but we must remember: he is asking us to believe that a large group of island residents, operating together in deceit, has falsified a murder and is attempting to frame an innocent man for the crime, all for some minor slight. A young woman goes missing, and we are asked to believe in the existence of an elaborate, malevolent conspiracy, rather than in a simple, if awful, accident.

"And, again, we are to accept this narrative because of the history of Marcus Farwell—the *distant* history. Marcus has been living with us on the island for many years now. He came here a troubled adolescent, this is true, but has grown into a responsible, ethically-committed man. We are aware, Mr. Feldt, of his past. He led a criminal life before he came to us, but this does not damn him in our eyes, but rather impresses on us his will to change."

Kitt's victim-face is slipping. Holy fucking *shit* what has he stumbled into here? There were lots, big lots, on the other islands. Why did he have to pick the one run by a cult? Jesus Christ, are the doors locked from the outside, or something? Has he been chosen as tribute? Do they have, like, fucking stones in their pockets?

"Many of us who came to Peliatos did so to become better versions of ourselves; I would be surprised if that was not part of what brought you, too, to our enclave. Marcus is no exception. I know him well; he stayed with me for some time, once, when he first arrived on the island and had nowhere else to go. I knew of his past, but knew also that he would redeem himself if given the chance, and he has, many times over. His work in our community, all done with complete dedication, and, too, without material compensation, has touched all of us. No matter what his past, Marcus has been a blessing to us, here, in the present.

"Yet who among us wouldn't rather believe this story of deceit, as shocking as it is, than accept senseless, horrific death? I myself would choose your theory, if I could bring myself to believe it. But I cannot trust my judgement. We, and you, Mr. Feldt, are too close to this to know what to believe. This is why it is not in our power to decide on the truth. We appreciate your efforts, but please, be patient. Help will arrive, and, we can hope, all will be made clear. Until then, let us acknowledge how little we know."

"I know enough. This is insane. This is just so goddamn typical. What kind of game are you running here? Your delusions aren't going to hold up in court. I'm coming after all of you."

"Please, try to be calm. We owe it to everyone. This is our home, after all. You speak of our community as if you know us, but do you? Perhaps you don't know us—just as you do not know Marcus Farwell, and just as we do not know what happened in that early morning four days ago. We are strangers, here, brought together by an unpleasant circumstance outside of our control. You don't know us; we don't know you. This will change, in time. You speak of Marcus's past; but what is *your past*, Mr. Feldt?"

PART THREE: DEATH AND SURFING

CHAPTER ONE

WHEN LENA AND RALEIGH SAW IT, THEY didn't know what it was called; it was then nothing more than an structural feature, an elaboration of domestic space. But, even unnamed, it still was what it was: a widow's walk. She was to learn this eventually, and then the name, suffused with decades of accumulated sorrow and loss, of women, hovering in the air, scanning the horizon, waiting for the sails of the ship to bring home man or body or a folded flag—then, the name would fit. In time, she would do the belated research. Why was it, after all, that pre-war homes built close to the shore needed these parapets, these elevated balconies, lookouts built before their need? It was of course a fact of home building, a style, a fad, but what could one make of the flowering of these walkways from the stems of tall houses— houses destined for abandonment, for ruin, to become nearly empty, and then empty all at once? The term was both a verb, and a noun: *a widow's walk*. It described an action and a setting, a feeling and its infrastructure. What could one make of these structures outfitted so perfectly for their scenes of love and death? This was more than an ocean view. It was an arrangement of longing and loss into which Lena would eventually fall. She had cursed them with architecture.

In her arms, the coolness of the still-damp neoprene, as if he were already a corpse. The sound of the pickup's engine turning over, and the dust that came from the road. The trees covering him up at the base of the hill, and never seeing him again.

Could she have seen it happen, from up on her balcony? She doubted it. It was only a fantasy of extended vision. The deck pointed at the appropriate line of surf, but from that elevation, he would have been invisible. But she did look out, when the day was coming to an end and he was not yet back, but saw nothing but the white lines of the break, already going grey in the fading light. And then she called, even though she knew that his phone would be ringing to itself in the glove compartment of their truck. And then she waited, in the dark, until the deep unformulated unease turned to fear. And then she began to walk.

From the sides of the path, a chorus of frogs and katydids sung her along. She had done this before, on other occasions when he was off somewhere in the Chevrolet but she still had errands to run; but she had never done it in the dark, and by the time she was in the trees the darkness was total. She made her way slowly, by the groove of the double-track under her feet, down the steep course from cliffside to sea level, over the narrow bridge, and into the halogen street lights of the main road.

A passing car gave her a ride to the beach. A stranger, one of the last ones, someone from the north end of the island. He let her off at the fork, where the road turned to dirt, and for a minute or two after the car had pulled away Lena stood there, trying to will herself into believing that she was being ridiculous. Surely he had gone along with his friends, whomever was there in the water when the light had finally turned on them, early this time of year, and was now at the Spinnaker, shaking sand out of his hair, drinking something blonde and bitter. She would, of course, come to the end of the dirt road and find it empty, the beach as well, because everyone had called it in for the evening, had gone home. It was too dark to surf now. Of course. It was obvious. All there was to do was to make sure.

Still, she was frozen in this suspended state. Until she looked, he was still there; until she looked, he was gone. She had been given, she realized, the power to kill him, the power to change their lives, and she didn't want to exercise that power. Finally she stepped along, towards the beach, each footfall bruised and tender. There were no creatures singing anymore.

When Lena came to the end of the road, she saw the truck, a dark shape against the lighter dark of the sand and sky. She ran past it and onto the beach, where there were no fires burning, no people, not even the late night kids, and no trace of him. The water was black where it hadn't been chopped up into foam, and lit close to the shore by tumbling bars of phospherescence. She called his name, and heard nothing but surf.

Lena returned to the truck. The keys were where he always put them, according to the surfer's worry of losing things in the deep; she took them from on top of the driver's side front tire and unlocked the door. The inside of the Chevrolet smelled like salt and sweat. His wetsuit wasn't there in the back seat, where he would have left it; his wallet, glasses, and phone were still in the glove compartment. She put them on the passenger seat, turned on the headlights, and waited. When it was well past midnight, when she could put it off no longer, she called the police and reported Raleigh missing.

At daylight they combed the length of the beach, looking for anything—Lena wouldn't let herself think, *body*, but finding a surfboard would have meant the same thing. She dialed every number in his phone and, to the ones that answered, was forced to tell a story that accreted, conversation by conversation, into a firm and fatal narrative. No one had seen him that afternoon, on the beach, in town, in any of the few places that, on a small island, each individual criss-crossed many times over each day. She called each store, the gas station, the town hall, the market, and the houses of all of their friends, and was told he wasn't there. And with this gradual, piece-by-piece erasing of his presence on the map, it became more and more impossible for him to be anywhere else but in the ocean. Lena knew the currents, knew that if he fell in the water at six o'clock he'd be far out in the gulf by nightfall. The Coast Guard also knew this, and sent patrol boats out; she waited as they covered all of the likely, and then unlikely, and then desperately unlikely stretches of the channel. She sat on the beach, feeling the sleepless night and the panic as it broke off and rounded out the edges of her world. She gave up before the Coast Guard did, returned to the empty truck, and drove back up to her home up high on the ridge.

The two of them had renovated it together, years ago, the house that they knew was right as soon as they saw it, coming up the switchbacks in the dusty Chevrolet with the radio on and the light flooding warm through the break in the trees. A home in the sky, with an unbroken view of the ocean from the wraparound deck. She shut all the blinds, turned off the lights, and lost twelve hours.

Lena couldn't decide whether she wanted them to find him or not. She knew that at this point Raleigh was gone, had to be gone by mathematical fact. What does one do in this situation? She didn't know the names of his parents, or whether they were still alive. She had met none of his family. She went through each drawer in their home, looking for something, a photo album, an address book, but found nothing. In the middle of the night she screwed a fresh tank into the propane lantern, took it outside to the deck that skirted the house, and, without knowing why, paced the perimeter along the rain-worn boards until the white flame guttered and the birds began to call back and forth to one another.

CHAPTER TWO

WIN IS IN LENA'S TRUCK; SHE'S BORROWED it to go into town to get groceries. She knows she's not supposed to drive with her leg in a cast, but it's five minutes away, and who cares; she can work the pedals alright, and the roads around here are nearly always empty. Plus, she's starting to feel like even more of a burden on Lena, if that's possible, sending her off with grocery lists. Making your host-slash-saviour dinner means a lot less when they have to fetch the ingredients.

The impromptu staycation at Lena's means that Win is finally cooking again, something she hadn't been able to manage around the scrubber's ten-to-seven-and-beyond schedule. She had traded that for takeout, and the kitchen in her open-concept apartment was coated in a layer of dust. She hadn't acclimatized to the late nights and, after a while, doubted she ever would. Before she was scrubbing, she was working out of her apartment doing touch-ups for a wedding photography conglomerate; a truly weird job. She'd get the photos, usually in the two to three hundred count, and get to work applying warming filters, fixing blemishes, whitening teeth, even, when she grew bored, cleaning up backgrounds, tucking in shirts, opening closed eyes. The eye part was the weirdest for a while, especially since nobody acknowledged, or even seemed to notice, that she was doing it—not even the clients, which meant that either, one, Win was doing a better job copy-pasting in eyes from other photographs or, often, from stock images, or two, that nobody actually knew the details of their loved ones' faces. Though now Win, at least, did, after staring through a pixel-grid at an imported hazel eye, blurring the edges out with measured strokes of her tablet pen. She became all too familiar with the contours of simulated mirth, of the increasing tension that built in the furrows of fake-smiling faces, especially that of the bride and groom, over the course of a shoot. Win spent an hour of collage work removing a photo-album-ruining tic from the face of, it looked like, the uncle of the bride—a tongue through parted teeth and upper-lip sneer that was probably not on purpose, a facial glitch that Win had to remedy by hunting through the full album for a photograph in which the man wasn't doing it. She copied this version into a new file, warped and skewed the mouth until the perspective matched, and then laid it over each other photo, adjusting for light. Win wasn't paid by the hour, and this kind of thing lost her money hand over fist, but she couldn't stop.

When the job posting went up for the scrubbing gig—well, the position was actually *Post-Intake Image Processing Assistant*—Win was one of the first applicants. The job was something like a dream gig for her. For starters, the stakes were satisfyingly high. It was a national, possibly international, operation, collecting images of all major urban centres across the country, and her job would be protecting the privacy of the people in those images—not, as she was before, buffing up their vanity. It also paid three or four times what she was making now. But the main draw was simple: Win was sick of working from home, sick of the isolation that was her old new normal. She had done a four-year interactive arts degree in three years, was streamlined right into a master's degree, finished that, and realized that she hadn't really seen anyone since her freshman orientation. She moved out of her dorm room and into an apartment in an unfamiliar city, in an unfamiliar country, on an unfamiliar continent. She got the wedding-photo-fixing job, paid her rent, and lived in a t-shirt and underwear for a year and a half. She learned how to talk down an overdue bill, how to spatchcock a chicken, and learned, too, that after a lifetime of seeing themselves in mirrors, brides and grooms will find their photographs uncanny and unflattering unless you flip the images horizontally.

AND THEN SHE GOT A JOB ERASING FACES. WIN bought some new clothes, wore them to work her first day, then recalibrated down a few levels of formality. The other new hires, her fellow PIPAs, were from similar backgrounds, give or take a few degrees of separation from the more comp-sci side of things. For the first time in years, Win had coworkers, not classmates, and, in the absence of competition—everyone was on the same pay grade, and the flood of images coming in daily was so massive that no one was fighting over work—they got along well. This was important, because they were to spend a lot of time together. Not so much outside of work, but at work, in shifts that could stretch to twelve hours, the eleven of them giddy and high on caffeine and overtime pay, churning out terabytes of processed images until they had emptied the inbox and could go home for the night.

And it was almost always night when she got off work, clocking out and trudging to her car, her brain gauzy with energy drinks and screen-time. Most days she'd swing through the cluster of takeout restaurants at the edge of the complex and grab some of whatever to half-eat on her drive home. She hadn't cooked for herself since getting the job, unless you counted reheating commute-cooled lo mein as cooking. It was a drag, the only downside she could think of to her days' late start and prolonged finish, and it was only partially compensated by how much of an income she was pulling in. Within eight months, she had paid off what was left of her student loans, tossed out her ratty second-hand furniture, and still had enough side money to systematically hit every upper-tier restaurant in town. When she flew back to Taiwan for Christmas with her family, it was, for once, not on the charity of her parents—which made her feel better about her visit home being a stopover on the way to a week and a half in Thailand.

WIN VACATIONED LIKE PAC-MAN WOULD, IF HE GOT vacations. She landed at Bangkok, took the train across the Chao Phraya River, and ate her way westward, heading towards the mountains and the Myanmar border. The train tracks veered southwards at Ban Pong, and she followed them, staying in little hotels, eating under awnings at night markets, in little family-run joints, or standing up in the street. As she drew further south, the character of the food changed, the eggy sweet-sour noodle bowls and green curries giving way to less friendly dishes, curries whose coconut milk, turmeric-tinged to an emergency yellow, did nothing to mitigate the insane levels of bird's eye chili. Win had meals that, on first bite, shocked her mouth entirely numb. She sat and sweat it out in cramped restaurants, her eyes and nose running like a grotesque fountain, and lay in bed hours later with her ears flushed and her scalp still tingling. In the morning she'd be planning out the day, finding the next spots, then hoofing it to the train station where she'd drink cups of coffee that were teeth-shakingly strong and thick as honey. By the time she had made it to the airport just north the Malaysian border, Win had built up enough of a tolerance that her pre-flight food court dinner, an allegedly red-hot khao pad, didn't even register.

Back at home, she did some digging around and found a market that sold the little red chilies, bought a plastic-wrapped package of them, and started trying to reverse engineer some of the dishes. But then her paid time off ran out and she was back to the whatever-food of the business complex mall, the late night Tex-Mex and heavy, Cheeto-orange butter chicken.

On weekends she'd drag coworkers to restaurants with tasting menus. First her fellow scrubbers, then, when their interest waned, she'd bring her new friend: Ana, one of the drivers she'd met at a company party. She didn't seem very ecstatic about the food, but she never said no when Win called to invite her out. And Win liked her, liked Ana, and the way that when you talked to her it felt like she focused on you and nothing else on the planet. She seemed lonely, too, and Win felt good to take care of that, liked being someone's only friend, especially when that friend was her only one, too. It worked.

PELIATOS MARKET IS TINY, THE SIZE OF A CORNER store, but instead of freezer pops and hot dogs they have an almost overwhelming amount of produce. She can see by the labels on the wooden crates that most of it is from Peliatos itself, and the rest is from the neighbouring islands—crazy green sprays of chives and ramps, knobbly sweet potatoes with soil still stuck to them, bunches of wine-purple carrots, and shallots the size of a fist. Win didn't come here with anything in mind, and now she realizes that was a mistake. She navigates the aisles—horrified that she's going to catch her crutch-end on something and bring the whole place down—until she comes to a cooler chest that looks like, and probably is, something from someone's garage. Under the lid is a bed of ice, and on that ice, an array of clams, mussels, and oysters; the air that wooshes out smells so much like the sea that it's like Win has stuck her head underwater.

It's a big dinner tomorrow: Lena's friend is coming by in the morning to pull the van out of the trees, and Win wants to mark the occasion.

CHAPTER THREE

KITT SLAMS THE DOOR OF THE SUV SHUT AND reverses out of the lot, and once he's out on the road he pulls out his phone and makes two calls. The first, to his lawyer, goes to voicemail; the second, to his dealer, doesn't connect. The phone banks off of the dash and lands somewhere in the back seat. *What the fuck was that?* Nothing that was supposed to happen, happened. He was told to expect a friendly audience; he walked into a buzz saw. This was supposed to be a straightforward thing—at least his lawyer said—you go in, you plead your case, you win their sympathy, you leave. He was pleading to a brick wall. It was his mistake. He didn't expect that the higher-ups at town hall would be, well, just more squatters, more delinquents, more island hillbillies immune to reason. The whole of Peliatos had drunk the Kool-Aid. He was fucked.

What a clear view of the smallness of the community: no matter what evidence he could bring against his accuser, no matter what he could provide to support himself, they listen, nod, and then side with their own. Their hero.

Back at the cabin, Kitt opens his laptop, hits the keys until it wakes up, and punches into a web search bar, "marcus farwell peliatos defenders." And there he is, or at least an article about him. In the island's shitty little newspaper, no less.

THE PELIATOS PROSPECT, JUNE 17 2009
MARCUS FARWELL, DEFENDER OF PELIATOS

When the tides of change came upon our island we didn't know where to turn or who to turn to, but someone rose up from our midst and came to our collective aid. That someone is Marcus Farwell, twenty-four years of age, a newcomer to Peliatos but is, we're glad to hear, already planning to be an old-timer. Mr. Farwell, who came for the surf but stayed — and how he stayed — for the people of our island, helped lead a revolutionary counterattack against Windermere Enterprises, the resort giant and international megapolis that had planned to build a massive, high-end luxury hotel on our precious and untrammelled island. Farwell, along with an inspiring number of our island's youth, led a multi-pronged protest against the development. They chained themselves to the diggers that would fracture our land; they picketed the corporate headquarters of Windermere Enterprises, and, under the leadership of our young saviour, staged a full occupation of the ferry to keep the construction crews from bringing over their tools of destruction.

It is true that, though an island and a proudly independent community, Peliatos is nonetheless subjected to the depredations of developers and their cronies-in-law, the regional and federal government; it is true that, despite the heroic efforts of Marcus Farwell and the rest of our island's young men and women, the resort development did go through — but were it not for these efforts, the resort would stand on twice as much land, would have destroyed twice as much of our virgin and protected rainforest, and for what: a sprawling complex of indoor and outdoor tennis courts which, if you ask this reporter, Windermere and its clients can learn to do without. Thanks to our young heroes, this addition was scrapped. If the big corporations will not listen to our words, Marcus Farwell and his fellows-in-arms have shown that, with their bodies and lives on the line, we can prevail.

Marcus has vowed to continue protesting the development, as well as any that follow in the future, and

it is our duty in repayment to his
efforts to never let him be without
our helping hands.

KITT STANDS UP AND FEELS, IN HIS HEAD, AN ALMOST
audible *click*. So he's the latest target, the new evil to be
rooted out. This was in the background of everything. He
could feel it in the attitude of the council, but even before
that, the baristas, the ferry ticket vendor, even the real
estate agent—a slight, subliminal shittiness in the way they
treated him that let him know he was *persona non grata*.
He knew what to expect, doing what he was doing here.
He had planned for some friction, knew that his development application would probably be filed last, knew that
the building permits would be an uphill battle. He had
weathered the bureaucratic passive-aggressive shit earlier
on, before the property was finally his, and thought that
was that. Did he celebrate too soon? And now this kid, this
anarchist activist hometown hero, has come at last to try to
fuck him over. And successfully, it seemed.

What would have happened, if he wasn't on the
property that night—would they have torched the place?
Tampered with the machines? He doubts it was as simple as a sit-in; there weren't enough of them to do much.
Was Marcus just there to fuck with him, mess with his
head, show him that he couldn't keep them from doing
what they wanted to? Kitt had the sense that, juvie asshole or not, Marcus knew what he was doing, and that
maybe the whole scene, his reaction to it, was part of the

overall plan—that the less Kitt co-operated, the better. The council was a set-up. Marcus knew that they'd unite against him. And even more if he let it handle itself, if he wasn't there to interfere with their rhapsody. The absent puppet master, pulling the strings. Maybe he was back at the construction site, with no one there, snooping around. Getting some new shit ready for him. Fuck. Kitt knew that sabotage would never really be out of the question. They would keep pushing him, Marcus and his friends, taunting him, knowing that he could do nothing. Now that he had seen how united the island was against him, and now that they knew he knew this, they could act with impunity.

Marcus accuses him of murder, or at least manslaughter, reckless endangerment, whatever, knowing that he can bank on the faith of his island sweethearts, and more importantly, knowing that no matter the accusation the default opinion would be, fuck the outsider, cast him out. Marcus could have accused Kitt of genocide and the town would nod their heads, at least until the police came, the actual police, not this station-wagon-driving sheriff. There was something cultish, something us-versus-them, about the council, about that woman, and the whole island. Well, that would be coming to an end, soon enough. The outside world was coming.

But when the feds come, what then? How sure can he be that the islanders won't continue the charade, for that's what it is: he doubts more than a handful of them actually *believed* that the girl was buried in his foundation, if the girl existed at all. Maybe the naïve ones, the rubes. Nothing in what his lawyer found said anything about a sister, but it wasn't like they cared at all for facts. This wasn't about facts; it was about attack and response, about attrition and irritation. Well, he's not about to take it; he is going to fight back. It doesn't matter how much shit they try to mobilize against him. He doubts they have his resources; he had a very good year, sales-wise; he can afford to throw some litigation around. But how long will they hold out? How long can *he* hold out? God knows that the rush job on building this place has already set him back. And every day he isn't allowed to work will rack up costs. He only knows what he needs to know for the sake of design, but he has a general sense of what will happen if the concrete fully cured before the moulds are taken off and the steel brackets bolted in. They'd have to take it all apart, and start again. They've got him working against the clock, hemorrhaging money. He realizes that this is the point, that the stall tactics were designed to cause exactly this kind of loss. They couldn't stop him outright; they'd have to wear him down. Death by a thousand papercuts, by a never-ending barrage of bureaucratic and legal bullshit.

But, fuck it; this is bigger than that. He'd let some people go, close a couple of the stores. This is a matter of justice. Who cares if he turns the island against him. It's not like he was here to make friends. In the end, once the house was built, his interaction with the island would be nil. He was only going to be here on the weekends, anyway. Unless, you know, shit on the mainland heated up in a big way and he had to make his escape—but then it would be *tabula rasa*, every man for himself, and he doubts that the people on the island would really survive in those conditions. He'd lock his doors, put up the gates, and ride it out. Fuck them. They deserved it, whatever they got. He almost wants that to happen, whatever it is, so he can watch them beg.

But of course, he'd need to get the house built first. Between him and that was Marcus Farwell, and whatever other hippies and deadbeats he had rallied together to help him with his cause. His "Defenders." *Jesus Christ.* What a joke. Let them try to bring him down. He'd sue them into oblivion. He knew the type—that as soon as things got real, as soon as they saw what they had gotten themselves into, they'd run like little frightened shits and stay out of his way. Then, he could finally be left alone, be able to go back to living life on his own terms. This whole situation, this clusterfuck, was an indignity, and he was ready to have it over with.

The council wanted to take it seriously? Fine, he'd take it seriously. In a few days, the real police would arrive and puncture the bubble that divided Peliatos from the real world. He trusts the feds, the city cops; they'll handle it. They're on his side, they've got to be; they'll know who he is and see through all of this hysteria. With the amount of taxes he pays, they're basically on his payroll. Still, could he trust the cops? A bigger question. Who knows. Every arm of the government was a load of shit. The delusion, the corruption, wasn't contained to Peliatos. After all, the Defenders had managed to fuck over the resort, at least partially. Surely the Windermere people had called in their own reinforcements, had relied on the rationality of law, and look what good it did them. He'd have to ready his own counterattack, and now, before things got any more official. He could get *ad hominem,* too.

Of course this kid is all over social media. Such a fucking amateur. Kitt opens up his profile, clicks through the
photos, and makes a sound of disbelief—there they are,
that night, in his house, or at least in the foundations of his
house, having their party. The images show them around
the campfire, drinks in hand, laughing, posing for the camera. What a nice night they're having. What fucks. What
insolent *fucks*. And they're caught on camera. But this
wasn't by accident, was it? It was smart to be documenting,
smart to be accumulating evidence. They were shitheads
and burnouts but they were doing the right thing, building
their own narrative. Or maybe they were just some idiot
kids having a good time, and it just so happens to work in
their favour. Look at their faces. What assholes. He keeps
clicking through—he can't believe how many photos there
are. In one of them, a kid is pissing against the wall of the
excavation, grinning over his shoulder. Kitt saves the picture to his desktop in case he sees this kid around. He'll
smash his fucking head in, or he'll press charges, or some
combination of the two. Pissing on his property. That'd be
easy. Public indecency. The fuck. He opens the window
back up, and clicks to the next picture. And then he stops.

The shot is strange, and the camera is fogged or blurred
out slightly, either from the smoke or from the phone itself.
It looks like it's been taken with one hand, stretched up
high; in the corner of the frame Kitt can see a pinkish blur
of a thumb near the lens. But that isn't important. It's out
of focus, but not enough. Kitt can see, lit up by the flash,
a body curled up in an all-weather sleeping bag, lying at
the bottom of one of the wooden enclosures. No. No, fuck,

no. He opens the image in a new window, and zooms in. The bag is pulled up close to her chin, and her head is covered by a toque, but there she is. The photo is even tagged: Stephanie Farwell.

Kitt stalks around his cramped cabin, kicking through boxes of fabric samples, cardboard tubes of rolled-up blueprints, and takeout containers. He punches the walls, and screams out profanity until his voice is shot. From outside, you can't hear him; the insulation is that good.

CHAPTER FOUR

THE WINCH DRAWS ITS CABLE TAUT AND THE bumper holds. Ana had assumed that the tension would pull it clean off, which meant that they'd have to try to attach the chain to the axle, or around a wheel, and she didn't have much faith that those wouldn't be torn off, either. The extent of damage to the van wasn't clear; much of it was hidden by the branches that, bent back by the vehicle's sudden entry into the grove, pasted their leaves against the wet metal and glass. The van had started that morning, but whether it would drive was another matter entirely. What also wasn't clear to Ana was, once the van was out, what she was going to do—if it worked, if everything wasn't knocked out of alignment, if the fuel tank hadn't been punctured by the jagged broken-off trunks of the birch trees, what then? The mechanisms inside had been knocked around a bit, but it was the hard drives that had the worst of it, at least based on what Ana could see. But she could work with it, could figure it out; if the processor and the relay were intact, if the camera hadn't shattered in its case, she'd simply have to redirect the images to the surviving storage. She'd have to re-record what she had of Peliatos so far, capture again whatever images were encoded on the busted disk. That was hardly anything, after all: the periphery of the island, or at least what they got before the accident. The accident.

When she had called work to tell them what had happened—a few days after the crash, and after Win had called in; Ana wanted to call in herself, too, to take some kind of ownership of the situation—she was probably audibly messed up on the painkillers but they still let her talk, first to her supervisor and then the coordinating officer. When they spoke they told her the same thing that they told Win: that above all else they were glad that she was safe, that all that was important to them was that they recuperate, and that she and Win had as much time as they needed to do so. They told her, kind of limply, that it was wasn't her fault. This was not true. It was Ana who was driving, she who had seen that thing—deer? coyote?—in the road, who had swerved, taken the van off of the highway and nearly killed both of them. True, anyone could have done this, but it wasn't anyone; it was her. Ana couldn't fix that, couldn't take back the event. She couldn't remove the spider-web of fractures in her closest and only friend's leg. But she could at least get the van out of the fucking trees.

Lena's friend signals from his rolled-down window. Ana steps back as, with the pulse of the truck engine and the snapping and cracking of the dogwoods, the van lurches towards the road. Another pull, and it's out of the trees and in the ditch. The truck reverses towards it and gathers up the slack in the winch chain. Ana walks through the shattered leftovers of the grove and waves to Win, who is on the road, single-crutched, watching out for cars. With the van no longer snared up in the trees, it's an easy job—the stonemason's giant truck pops back into first, crawls forward, and in an instant the van is up and on the road, perpendicular to traffic. Now she can get a good look at the van—it's sitting flat on its suspension, which means that the struts aren't bent out of shape, but the outside is scuffed and dented like it's been through a war zone.

Ana carefully scales the ditch and helps unwrap the chains from the van's rear bumper. She's able to do this now, though she has a harder time raising her hands above her head. They drop the coils of chain to the pavement and the man returns to his truck, where he turns on the winch. Ana watches as the chain is slowly drawn up into the spool, kicking kinks out of it with her foot. When the chain is clear she goes around to the unlocked driver's side door of the van and gets in. It had been raining for three days straight, and sodden leaves cake the windows and make the light in the van diffuse, brown-toned. She turns the key to the first click and the wipers, thick with plant matter, clear a milky patch of glass in front of her. Through it she sees the black rubber tracings of where the van went off the road, the torn grooves in the green grass, and at the end, the pulverized stand of trees. Beyond that, the cabin; Lena watches from the doorway. She turns the wipers up until they're working fast enough to fling off the clumps of leaves and hears, faintly, the sound of the truck as it pulls around her and drives off. Win or Lena's face appears in the cracked glass of the passenger window, she can't tell. She can hear them pulling on the latch but the door won't open. It's caved in, the interior plastic split and popped out of its fittings. She tries not to think of what would have happened if she hit the tree any harder, if the door was forced any further in. She tries not to run the simulation, but she can't stop it—the bent door crushing Win in her seat, coming in hard from her right side, her head's impact with the glass. The things the wedge of metal would have done to her ribs, her organs.

Ana becomes aware of a sound, a clockwork clicking slow and high up, and it takes her a few intervals to remember that it's the camera, awake and firing. She twists the key and the sound of the camera is lost in the rumble of the battered engine. Win comes around to her side, and Ana rolls down the window.

"I'm going to take it down the street and make sure everything's working. Do you want to come along?"

"Hell yes. Do you think it's safe?"

"Sure."

"I guess if it was going to explode, it would have already exploded."

"Well —"

"It's probably best if we don't think of it."

"Yes."

"Let's go."

CHAPTER FIVE

WIN HAS TO WAIT FOR ANA TO GET OUT first, and then she hoists herself up into the driver's seat. The cast makes crossing over the centre console annoying, and she's at the point where her leg doesn't even hurt and is just made useless by the cast. She wants the doctor to take it off, and she wants Lena or her friend to help her take the passenger-side door off, too, so she can get in the normal way, if they're going to be doing this again. Doing what? Win supposes that they're going to finish the island, though Ana has never said this outright. Win knows that Ana wouldn't want to leave the island without at least doing the job, and if this smashed-up and rattled van is up for it, then smashed-up and rattled Win is, too. She slides into to her seat with a groan, buckles in, and sees what she can do about the air bag. It's not a horror-show like Ana's, covered in nose-blood, god, *covered*, but it's in the way and annoying and a bad reminder, and she wants it gone. When Ana gets into her seat and shuts the door, Win has her hands full of the rough white nylon and is stuffing it back into the compartment as best as she can. There must have been some kind of lid, the piece of dash that the bag exploded through, but she can't find it anywhere, so she just crams everything in and hopes it stays. The busted plastic of the door is jabbing against her, and the glass looks like its ready to fall out entirely. Win feels sick being back in here, but with Ana in her seat, she can't exactly leave.

She looks at Ana. The plastic brace is off, traded for a soft foam ruff, and it's a good thing, or else Win would have no sense at all that time had passed. It's been, she thinks, two weeks—two weeks since they rode the ferry over to the island, two weeks since the accident. Two weeks leaning so hard on the charity of Lena, who has done so much for them. Win offered to pay her—they're taking up her guest room, have outnumbered her in her own house—but Lena waved the offer away. Win figures that she is getting something out of this, too; that she wanted to help them, that this was something she believed in doing. Win thought at first that she was just lonely, all by herself in that house by the ocean, but then, soon enough, she met all of Lena's friends. There's hardly been a day since they arrived—"arrived"—that there hasn't been someone who has popped in looking for Lena, or came through for dinner, or just to say hello to them, her mystery guests—a parade of all of these kind and weird hippies and surfers and naturopaths and artist-looking types. Win has the sense that Lena is the central hub of some big wheel of community, and is also just, at the base of it, a good person, the kind of person who attracts people. It breaks Win's heart that someone like that had to go through the loss that she had. Her, and Ana. All of these awful things happening to good people. Win's become less and less a fan of what life does to you. Herself included, though she's realizing lately that if her life has had a narration track it's in the *Wheel Of Fortune* voice, broken leg aside. This is, as far as she can remember, the only really bad thing that's ever happened to her.

Ana cranks the wheel to the left as far as it will go and hits the gas. The van lurches, more things falling out of their brackets onto the floor in the back, and turns into the lane. Win twists in her seat to see what's happened with the gear, but any new development is lost in the general mess. It looks, she thinks, like a downed plane—ribbons of loose wires, smashed chunks of plastic, bits of plant matter that got in who knows how. Seeing this makes her realize that maybe she was lucky to be alive, but that's not really a thought you want to hold onto.

THEY'RE GOING DOWN, PAST WHERE THEY HAD swerved off, as if they were simply resuming—as if two weeks ago they had just slammed the brakes, let the thing, whatever it was, pass them by, and continued along in their itinerary. But their room at the resort would have someone else in it by now, surely. And the van was beat to hell. The engine was making a worrisome knocking sound, especially when Ana pushed on the gas pedal, and even at idle it was running rough. She doesn't remember it being this loud in here before. The van sounds like how Win imagines an old lawn mower would sound. Maybe the muffler is broken, or something in the transmission has gone. This is the extent of Win's automotive knowledge. Pretty crude, but why would she need to know any of this—it's not like she's ever owned, or ever wanted to own, a car. Or been able to afford one. She always liked walking around anyway, which ... She guesses she'll have to wait and see how her leg heals. The doctors said she had a "displaced fracture." Meaning that the force of the impact that broke her leg did such a good job of it that the pieces were knocked out of alignment. They reset them at the hospital—good lord, the pain, even with all the sedatives they gave her—and it looked fine enough to not need pins or bars or struts screwed in, but future surgery was always a possibility depending on how well it mended. Win's not sure about how good of a job she's doing, in that respect; maybe if she could stay off of it. Oops. The couch potato act was getting boring, and Win wanted to, well, *do* stuff, to explore. And out of a probably unconscious resentment, she kept "forgetting" her crutch. The damage it was doing to her sweet and tender armpit didn't seem worth it. She's such an idiot. She left it leaning against a tree in front of Lena's and wasn't particularly looking forward to having to hop-hobble all the way back to the cabin without it if the van's engine did what it sounded like it wanted to do and bit the dust.

Through the busted window the light is glittery and prismatic, almost pretty despite the menace of that broken glass. They cruise down the narrow road, picking up speed as Ana tests things out, and the trees out of the windshield are wet and heavy with rain. Always the trees, everywhere, pine, fir, elm, birch, beech, every kind Win has ever heard of plus some. She would miss this, the insane green abundance, the way that all of the human elements of the island seemed tucked between boughs, fit between spaces wherever the forest allowed. Except for the road, she figures, which has been hacked right through all of this, who knows when. They should have left it all alone.

As they drive on, the knocking slows, then stops. The engine has apparently worked through whatever crisis it was having. The van is pulling a bit to the right, and it is louder, much louder, inside, but aside from that—and the smashed passenger door, and the blood on Ana's air bag, and whatever carnage was going on with the computer gear in the back—it doesn't seem to be in risk of exploding, at least. The camera is working, or at least firing, even. Win looks behind her seat again and sees, unbelievably, that some of the lights are still on back there, even with the computer's entrails pulled out and scattered all over the floor. Maybe they'd be able to salvage some of the gear before they crushed the van into a cube and sold it for scrap. Win would like to be the one who pushed the button. Maybe they'd give her fifteen minutes with a can of spray paint and a baseball bat, first. Or, more poetically, her crutch.

The van passes a clearing in the trees, a driveway, and Ana slows them down.

"Whoa. What is this?" Win leans forward to see out of the smudged-up windshield.

"Looks like another resort?"

Through the break in the trees is a vast opening, though less man-made than ordained by the massive, smooth rock that rippled and dipped its way to the ocean. If the clearing wasn't man-made, man had certainly made use of it: gouged into the rock is a deep hole, and rising out of it, a cage of wood and rebar partially filled-in with concrete. As they pull the van into the gravel drive, the shape of the structure becomes more clear: a long, squat rectangular box, stepped out here and there, big, not big enough to be a hotel, but too big to be a house. Or at least too big for a house by the standards of the island, which if it had a two-storey building, Win hadn't seen it. They pull up to the construction site, and Ana opens the door and slides out onto her feet. She's left the engine running, worried, she said, that if she kills it it won't start again. Win joins her, awkwardly scooting back over to the driver's side and lowering herself out, good leg first.

She hops over to where Ana is standing, near the edge of the pit.

"This is why we're here, right?"

"What do you mean?"

"This is the kind of stuff our company loves. Fresh terrain, new ground, catching the boom."

"Right. They know there'll be more of this soon. I wonder how fast?"

"Unless we drive the van into the ocean, never report back, probably, a year or two and this place will be all like this."

"You're kidding."

"Yeah, you're right. Even if we went rogue someone else would do it. Someone always has to lead the way."

"So this is the new warehouse district? The new industrial lot?"

It's prime real estate, with the shore right there, although you'd have to jump off the cliff to get to the water. Win supposes it was someone rich who finally got to build their dream house, someone who decided, for whatever reason, to do it here—and maybe rich people don't like to get wet. Who knows. Win's already been in the ocean a few times, with a garbage bag wrapped around her cast; they pulled a couple of lawn chairs out into the shallows in front of Lena's place and hung out there when the weather was hot enough. They're perched on the edge of the excavation, looking down, when from behind them they hear footsteps, coming fast. Suddenly there is a man behind them, his red face stubbled with grey, and his posture is all threat. Win grabs Ana by the arm and turns her around just in time.

CHAPTER SIX

K ITT SEES THEIR VAN FIRST—A PORTABLE scrap heap, total hippie fare, though surprisingly without a mural painted on its side—and slows his SUV to a stop behind it. He needs to be quiet. He leaves his lunch on the passenger seat and pulls out his phone, clicks open the camera. He moves carefully around the van, goes to look inside it, but the window is smashed up. There's no way this thing is street legal. He gets a picture of the licence plate. What was going down? He tries to remember whether or not he locked his cabin door, but they'd break it down anyway if they wanted in. What could they be after? Planting evidence, slashing tires, putting sugar in the gas tanks of his diggers, or, just waiting, waiting for him to come back. And then what? Would there be a whole gang? He should keep going, or he should get back in the car, go back to the hotel, call someone. He continues down the driveway.

There were two of them, two young women, at the edge of the site. Keeping watch? He's taking their picture when he sees the cast, the neck brace, and thinks: is this the next step? If they've halted construction, could they also get the whole construction site shut down, boarded up as a danger to the community? The nerve of these fucking people. He shoves his phone in his jacket pocket and runs to them before they can do whatever it is they're planning on doing.

"Listen, you delinquent fucks."

"Whoa—calm down, mister." The one with the cast.

"Who else is with you? Who's here?"

"We don't know what you're talking about, sir. If we're trespassing, we'll go."

"Now that you've finished, right?"

"Finished what? Look—okay we should really get out of here." She pulls on the other woman's arm, the silent one.

"Yeah, get the fuck out, you and your friends. And if you or your crew comes back here trying to pull some shit on me, I've got the whole place recording on camera."

"We weren't doing anything. We were just curious. We don't know what you're talking about." There is definite fear in her voice; good. Maybe that will translate into them leaving him the fuck alone. But he doubts it. They'll send more people.

"Curious, sure. Tell your leader, Farwell, I'm curious, too."

"Tell who?" The silent one speaks.

"Come on, Ana, let's go."

The two women back around him, putting Kitt between them and the pit, and then retreat across the gravel to their van—the one in the cast hobbling, really leaning into it. Maybe she was actually hurt, after all, her and the one with the neck brace. Who gives a shit. They get in the van, both through the driver's side door, slow and clumsy. Kitt wonders what the recruitment process is like for the Defenders, that would let these two in. Likely it's a volunteer gig, like the fire department and everything else on this piece of shit island. They back out of the driveway and pull onto the street and Kitt watches them go.

He misses his confidence, how sure he felt before the outlines of this total fucking mess became clear. He could deal with a pissing battle, had won many over the years. But this was bigger than that. It had started before he even knew it, started before he even arrived on the island, and now it was happening and he was losing control. It doesn't matter what he said to the two women; that they were here, at his home, was enough. He was full of shit; he doesn't have security cameras; all he's got are the pictures on his phone and those mean nothing, except for that they were here. Things haven't even started, and they've already won. He has pictures, sure, but their pictures are better.

It doesn't even matter whether the photo of the girl is staged, whether their story is true. Obviously Kitt hopes that the girl, whoever she is, wasn't dead. Sure. But it doesn't matter. They had him. Eventually, sure, the cops would find out; they'd take apart the foundations, they'd tear apart his whole construction site, soon enough. Maybe there's a dead girl, maybe there isn't. That wasn't the point. That could just be the beginning. How easy it would be for them to say, hey, two people were at Kitt Feldt's property and were injured by unsafe conditions at the construction site. Or they could break into his cabin and plant some foul shit on his computer. Incriminating emails. False documents. Child pornography. He knows this sounds insane, and maybe it is, but the fact is that even if this was their plan, they could do it. Anything they decided to put onto him would stick. They could wrap him and his project in red tape so thick he'd never see his way out, make him spend months and years bleeding out money trying to prove he's being had. They've already cost him a couple dozen thousand in construction setbacks, and there's no way that the investigation will start and finish quickly enough for him to not have to start over from scratch, with whatever wreckage is left. All while his construction crew backs out of their contract and is hired out to other bidders, and his brand, flying on autopilot in the hands of his creative directors, takes its inevitable nosedive. That was their aim—their jaded, cynical pragmatism. They couldn't stop the resort, that'd be impossible. They could only slow it down, attack it piecemeal, maybe cut it down in size by a fraction. It's the same. But it isn't. This wasn't some kind of partial measure; this was bigger than that. He could see it now, see the moves left to make, see his own failure. This time, they'd win. They could fuck him so badly that he'd have to vanish, he'd have to disappear. They could do whatever they wanted to him. They have him in the palm of their hand, they have him under their magnifying glass. He's is stuck in their narrative, now, racing against drying concrete.

Unless—unless unless unless.

He didn't need to sit on his hands while he waited, did he? He couldn't continue the construction, not with his crew on the other side of the channel, and any move he made against Marcus Farwell and his cronies would surely blow up in his face. The photograph, that sleeping girl, was the ultimate ammunition, the ultimate currency. But he wasn't entirely without a course of action. The simplicity, the brute material simplicity of it, is exhilarating. So he'll have to take down his foundations; so be it. Why not do that right now, and specifically, that famous section, that weight-bearing pillar poured with that unique mixture of concrete and hippie girl? He refuses to believe it, refuses to believe that this girl, somehow, wouldn't have, you know, *woken up*, that his crew wouldn't have thought to fucking check. It's got to be bullshit, but it's his word against theirs—or, in fact, his word against their photograph. Well, he'd get proof of his own.

He races over to the excavator closest to the edge of the pit, and climbs into its seat. The keys are in the ignition down by his feet; he's not sure why the crew left them in there—the liability, *jesus christ,* and how easy it would have been for Marcus or one of his hooligans to get in there and wreak hell—but maybe it's a good sign. But turning the rig on was the easy part. There are too many levers and switches in such a cramped space, and Kitt's gaze bounces from each to each, in search of at least one with a label. He flips up a row of toggles on the dash, and some lights come on. Yes. He tries the two bulky levers, like super-sized gearshifts, that seemed like the obvious choice. They don't budge. He hits more switches, then tries the levers again. Nothing. He's punching the dash, pushing buttons at random, when he sees out of the narrow windscreen a pickaxe leaning against a bin. He jumps out of the digger and runs over. It has a good heft, a good, old-school feel. *Hell yeah*. He throws it over the edge, grabs the ladder, and scales down into the pit.

The pillars of the foundations are immense and fill the space with the deep funk of wet wood and fresh cement. He grabs the pickaxe and catches his breath. He's able to get the plywood off of the base of the mould using the tip of the axe as a wedge, pushing against it with the handle against his chest until the nails pop loose. Once he's gotten it started, it's easy; he grabs the edge of the sheet of wood and walks it backwards, the fasteners straining and creaking until the whole thing comes loose. The rest of the panels come off easily, and then the base of the pillar is bare. He feels the smooth damp surface of the concrete, then tentatively swings the axe at it. With a meaty, solid *thwack* the tip sticks in. He pulls it out and swings again, this time knocking loose a fist-sized chunk. If he had tried this a week from now it would have been fully dried, or cured, whatever, and it would be like chipping away at a boulder. Instead, the texture is like art-class clay. He takes off his jacket, rolls up the sleeves of his shirt, and gets to work.

The handle of the pickaxe is soon slippery with a paste of sweat and grey muck. Each time the blade contacts the concrete, little gritty clumps splatter out and get on his arms, his face. He's trying to get a sense of what will happen when he's carved out enough of the base—it seems to be getting softer as he gets deeper, and maybe at a certain point he'll be able to simply push the thing over from the other side, like a huge sandcastle. There's some danger in that. The pillar isn't that wide—about four feet on each side—but it's tall enough and definitely heavy enough to crush him, so every few swings he stops, looks up, then continues, his arms and back throbbing, like some kind of Brutalist post-industrial lumberjack.

An hour in, he's attacked the base of the block on three sides, and the texture of the concrete is changing. Is he getting to the gooey centre? He's trying not to think about how much easier this would be with the digger, or with a jackhammer, or even a chainsaw. Or if he had some friends to help him. No such person on the island, however. The exertion and the musty stink of the concrete is giving him a pounding headache, but he pushes on, swinging the pickaxe overhead, feeling the wet thud of contact in his aching hands, pulling the blade free, and raising it up over his head again. He gives it one more whack, and then drops the pickaxe. He leans against the block and thinks he can feel it shift. Yes. He goes around to the back of the pillar, and pushes as hard as he can. Nothing happens. He shifts his footing, plants his shoulder against the block, and tries again. Of course nothing happens, this is fucking *concrete*. He steps back around and realizes, he's barely made a dent. It looks like some disinterested beaver came by, had a few bites, then moved on, and that was after hours of back-breaking work. The deeper he gets, the more difficult it's getting. The concrete is sticky and waterlogged, dense as a brick of cream cheese, grabbing the pickaxe blade and not letting it go. He'd be here all day, all week, trying to knock down this pillar of rock. What is he thinking? What is he doing?

But, more importantly: what else does he have to do? *Fuck it.* Kitt reaches down and lifts up the pickaxe. Swings. Pulls it out and dislodges a wet clot. He knocks the pickaxe against the rock wall to get the stuff off of it, and swings again, grunting against the impact. He's having to lean back, one foot against the pillar, to get the axe out, and the coarse grit coating the handle is making a lacerated mess out of his hands, but *whatever*, keep going, keep going. He gets it free of the gummy mass, raises it over his shoulder, swings, makes contact, his hair plastered to his forehead, his eyes and the corners of his mouth encrusted with little globules of cement, his clothing slick with it. Pull, lift, swing, connect. Pull, lift, swing. He spits a grey blob of grit and wipes his mouth. He hacks away, again and again, and then something catches—he can't get the pickaxe out, it's stuck, really stuck this time, and when he leans and pulls back against it with all his weight it gives a little, but something is holding it fast, and when he lets go and crouches down he sees that looped around the pickaxe blade is the strap of a backpack.

CHAPTER SEVEN

W IN WATCHES ON THE TELEVISION AS THE excavation team takes the pillar apart. It's her third or fourth time seeing the recording; it's all the station is playing. They start from the top, scooping away the concrete, first with the bucket of a backhoe, and then, as they dig deeper, with jackhammers and finally with hand-held tools. When they find her, the camera feed goes black. Win learned the rest by looking around online.

The girl had made her way into the plywood enclosure late that night, looking for somewhere out of the wind to sleep. Work started before sunrise the next day, and, when the sound of the machines starting up didn't wake her, the pouring concrete did. Did she scream for them to stop? Would they have heard her over the sound of the high-bore pump? The investigators did know that she woke up, and that she tried to get out—climbing against the current of thick muck as it filled up the enclosure. They know this because of how they found her. The diggers, working through the still-congealing sludge with their tools, had made their way down through three or four feet of the block. They were skeptical, had almost given up and declared the thing a hoax. Then came a shout from one of the excavators—she had found a hand, a human hand, outstretched towards her. There is a split-second shot as the camera operator zooms in, an image of the hand, fingers and palm white against the grey concrete, and then the video cuts out.

After the video feed went dead, after the hand, the excavation took on a more frantic aspect. All present grabbed whatever tools they could find and pulled away at the setting concrete. So then they knew, could at least extrapolate the details. She was lying there, likely asleep, and then the cascade of concrete from above. She frantically tried to get out, but it was impossible under all of that weight; the dense slush smothered her, then bore her up as the chamber filled, lifting her from the bottom of the pit. The currents of sticky liquid rock, settling and growing denser as the air was crushed out of it, this ooze, had carried her up and up into the centre of the pillar. It looked like she was swimming, she *was* swimming, trying to claw her way out, but it was all coming in too fast. She made it halfway up before she lost consciousness. And then the enclosure was full, full of several hundred pounds of cement around and on top of her.

With that column finished, the workers turned off the spout, scraped the top of the block smooth, and moved on to one of the other enclosures. This, this part is the most horrible thing of all for Win: that the workers were down in the foundations, walking among the moulds, talking amongst themselves, tapping them to test for air bubbles, while inside one of them the girl was encased like an insect in thickening amber. Then Win remembers, with a shudder, that *she* was there, too, earlier today—standing above the scene, looking down, while the girl, suffocated and immobilized, reached up.

THE THREE OF THEM, WIN, ANA, AND LENA, WATCH the coverage together, then, on the computer in Lena's office, they look at the news reports as they come in. There are more photographs, and links to the broadcast: the hands of the workers, scraping away with their tools, and then the yell, and then the quick zoom. There are other videos too, shots of Kitt Feldt, the man who had approached and threatened them, who had met with Lena and the rest of the council at the town hall. In these videos—shots of him at the site on the day of the excavation; him at his room in the hotel, being interviewed—the rage that Win saw on his face is gone and replaced with a complete lack of animation, like the face of a sleepwalker. It was his home, his construction site, and somehow also his construction company, even though he was some kind of fashion tycoon. He's facing potential charges of criminal negligence, but he doesn't seem to respond to any of this, at least not in a way the cameras can pick up. Lena says that the charges will probably be dropped by the family, as they didn't really see the point, and the whole situation was too convoluted to play well in court. But the municipality had other ideas. They were going to sue him for damages, maybe even charge him for manslaughter. They'd definitely axe his permits and make sure he never came back to the island. This is how these things go, Win supposes, but would any of this really help? Is that really what justice is? Besides, it looks like he has money to spare, and in the end that's all that would matter.

Eventually they see everything there is to see and the three of them return to the house. The television is still on. The local channel is replaying one of the interviews, the one with Marcus Farwell, the girl's brother, and Ana and Lena sit and watch. It's almost midnight, the whole day having passed by in a kind of video daze, and they haven't eaten since the lunch they had when the guy arrived to help them get the van out of the trees. Win clomps into the kitchen, grabs the canvas bag of mussels from the fridge, and empties it into the sink. With the faucet on, she can't hear the TV, but she's watched the interview a couple of times now. Marcus, who Lena says she knows, it was his sister. He was there the night before it happened. He went to the man, Kitt Feldt, and told him, but Kitt didn't believe him. The police did, though. Believe him, that is. Win can't imagine what that would have been like, how that would have felt—your sister has been killed, and you know it, and who did it, but they won't listen to you. And then the person who did it accuses you of fraud, or extortion, or whatever it was, and you're having to fight against this whole huge thing while your sister's just died, or you think she has, but you can't even find the body. The interviewer asks Marcus if he has anything to say to Mr. Feldt.

The mussels clack together like stones as Win washes them, the water from the tap hand-numbingly cold. She's going to do something simple, fettuccine con cozze, with pasta she got fresh from the market. The propane stove clicks and lights, and she takes down one of the hanging copper pans. Oil, medium heat, then the garlic and chili, and then the mussels clatter in and make the oil pop and spit. Win pours some white wine in and the steam comes rushing up towards her. The shells are closed tight; when they open, they're ready.

With the faucet off, Marcus's voice comes back into the kitchen. He's answering a question about the night, when he and his friends, and his sister, were at the construction site. *Did you do anything to provoke Mr. Feldt, to make him suspect you of foul play. Yes. We were on his property after all, only we didn't know he was there. So you didn't think he'd find out. Yeah, exactly. We were just using it for the night. Using it?* The second burner flicks on, and she nudges open the tap with the back of her hand to fill the pot. *We were just looking for a place to crash.* She scoops salt out of the salt well, drops it into the water, then digs around the cupboards for the lid. She looks up and sees Ana, her foam cuff off, the back of her head. *We didn't want any trouble.*

The news station goes to commercial. A teenage boy is getting up in the morning—he's in a hurry. He pulls jeans on off of the bedroom floor, wriggles into a shirt. This kid is gross. He grabs his backpack, ducks into the bathroom, then slides across the kitchen floor and intercepts a perfectly-aimed granola bar courtesy of mom. He shimmies out the door, to, ostensibly, middle school, high school, wherever. He's brushing his teeth with his finger as he walks. With his finger. The granola bar appears on screen. The water in the pot starts to boil. Win turns away from the TV and opens up the package of pasta—the fettuccine is thick, ribbony, gritty with the semolina that it sheds when it hits the water. When she turns back towards the television, Marcus is there, standing in the living room. Lena is with him, and Ana is getting to her feet. Marcus is shorter than he looked on television, a few inches shorter than Win, but he has the physique of someone who spends a lot of time in the ocean. Lena puts a hand on his arm and directs him towards the kitchen.

"Win, this is Marcus."

"Hi, Marcus—I'm so sorry." Win feels like an idiot, but doesn't know what else to say.

"Thanks."

"Marcus is going to have dinner with us, if that's alright."

They leave the kitchen and Win drains the pasta, tosses it with the oil and garlic and mussels in a stoneware bowl, shaves some parmesan on top. She brings it out and, rounding the corner, sees Marcus on the couch, bent over. He's sobbing with fast, hysterical breaths, crying like a little boy, and Lena is cradling him in her arms with her head bent to his. Win feels like she's swallowed something large and heavy. She puts the bowl down on the table, takes a step towards them, changes her mind, and clomps back to the kitchen. Ana's there, standing by the fridge and looking, well, unsure. Win puts an arm around her, scoots her out of the way, and grabs the bottle of wine out of the fridge. Ana collects some cutlery from the drying rack, and the two of them walk back in together. Marcus is sitting up now, murmuring something to Lena, who's nodding, saying something back. When they see Win and Ana they get up and join them at the table. The wine is alright—a bit sweet, a bit too desserty—but the fettuccine is, all things considered, a hit.

CHAPTER EIGHT

IN LENA'S DREAMS THERE ARE COUNTLESS WAVES, but they are all iterations of the same one. The one that took him—if there was one, if he did not simply slip, concuss his head against a rock, come tumbling down with the weight of the water on him. She put a lot of thought into this at first, had had to in the conversations with the police and friends and family; and so, each night, it came to her. In how many ways could it have happened? There were no predators, no orcas here, even out past the break; the currents diminished their food supply, and they'd be kept away from the remnants by the boat traffic, what little there was. There were crabs, some small saltwater fish, and some seals—but nothing savage enough to take down Raleigh. There was some small comfort in this, that he did not die in the jaws of some creature. And so, barring that, a kind of equation held: he was too strong a swimmer to drown from being swept out by a rip current, too competent a surfer to have gone too near to the rough rocks at the border of the beach; therefore, he died from a wave. A freak wave, the multiplication of oceanic math that Lena knew well and he did too, something rough-edged and sudden, its surface backtracking into the whorl of the barrel, something to catch him off guard, to bring the board out from underneath him and, in an instant, pull him down into the churning water. Perhaps he hit his head against the surfboard, not too hard, hard enough to put him out, and then the rushing water from the shore sucked him out into the deep. All of this in hardly even a moment, just a feeling, suddenly off-balance, knowing that there has been a mistake, then a white rush of froth, being thrust under, then blackness. His body, far out, in the middle of fifty feet of water. The quiet pull of the current, his long and beautiful hair haloed out around his head. She could tolerate this last image.

No one was with him. He never surfed alone, but this time he had. Though it would not have helped, even if his friends were there—he would have been too far out, the event invisible amidst the foam and spray. If they had been there, and if they had seen, and if they had swam out as fast as they could, it still would have been too late. If she were there, on the shore—she sometimes would come out, if she was done work for the day, and watch him, sitting and talking with whomever was out of the water at that moment—she still couldn't have saved him. She would have watched him go under, and then waited for him to resurface. Of course she would liked to have been there, to be with him for it, but it would have made no difference. She wouldn't have known what she was seeing: just a second above the water, the board coming out in the cross-cutting rip, and then plunged below. But she wanted to have seen the wave, seen it in waking life, and not just in dreams.

He is in the water, belly down on his surfboard, paddling out. The sun is on his back, drying the seawater into a prickling sheen of salt. Heat on his neck and shoulders; the cool of the ocean up his arms. He's heading towards the wave. It's building against the horizon, a fat blue bar of fast-moving water, still somehow holding back from the break, rolling in a giant sinusoidal swell. He'll have to get on the other side of it, let this one pass him by—up and over, over the hump, the peak. He feels the dip at the front of its rising edge, a fractional loss of gravity, and then he's coming up it, his surfboard pitching back along the curved sheet of water, and still going, further and further towards vertical—first five, then ten, then fifteen feet, and still the wave is sucking him up and into its swirling face. He's gripping onto the sides of his surfboard so he doesn't slip off, doesn't fall back into it, and the wave carries him up, high above the waterline and into the dazzling sunlight. At last he is at its crest, still flattened on his stomach, but somehow the wave is still coming, still building underneath him, lifting him up towards the sky. Finally, he comes over the crest, and Raleigh sees below him an abyss, a massive, cliff-like drop of absent water. The ocean on this far side is emptied, clipped off by an invisible wall, falling into a chasm six hundred feet deep. He cannot slow himself down, can't keep the water from carrying him over the edge; he plunges his arms and legs in but the force is too strong. He looks down, below the nose of his surfboard, at the dry seabed. It is littered with dessicated fish like specks of silver foil, with the stunned and still bodies of whales—and then the water drops out from underneath him and he's falling, screaming, falling.

WHEN LENA WAKES UP, SHE IS SITTING UPRIGHT IN her bed, her feet on the floor, apparently about to stand. Where would she be going to? She tries to let the dream carry her, past the interruption, and follows it to the window. She pushes back the damp strands of hair that are stuck to her face and looks out, and it is the view from the old home: the rich dark green of the treeline ramping down to the grey-blue of the water, the familiar frame of the clearing, the white arcs of gulls like floating paper. Then the image fades, and she's left facing the darkened square of glass.

Lena moves through the quiet of the bodies sleeping in her house. It is early, early morning, and they won't be up for hours yet, but she knows she won't be able to fall back to sleep. Marcus is on the couch, and as she moves past him towards the kitchen, she reaches a hand out to pass over the bulge of his shoulder beneath the blanket. She wasn't expecting him here last night, or at least only was in a general sense—he was always welcome, and her home was forever open to him or to his friends. They usually did not come, were content camping or squatting or drifting through the living rooms of their own demographic. And so was Marcus, until now. When Lena thinks of his sister she feels a pain too sharp for so early in the day, and she quickly thinks about other things. This new crisis had, in a way, brought time back into her household, broken the prolonged spell of the fifteen days that had suspended the two girls in her life, and she was sad to think that they would be leaving soon. For they surely would—what else was there for them to do? They were mobile, Ana's neck nearly healed, Win up on crutches, and their van was out of the trees and on the road and appeared to be in working condition. Lena is glad to have helped them, to have done what she was able to do, and had enjoyed their company. The quiet, interior Ana, behind whose hesitations and retractions pulsed a flow of urgency and feeling, and Win, Winfried, that odd name, one from Lena's university days—and one that, as she was delighted to discover, was self-elected. *Winfried*: a German boy's name chosen by a ten-year-old Taiwanese girl. Win had done most of the talking, and Lena has the sense that this was the dynamic of their relationship: the output and input, the sender and receiver.

Much of what she knew of Ana was through inference, from watching her interactions, but Win did not make you guess. From the day when the pain had subsided enough for her to come out of the sedation, Win was a nearly constant conversational companion for Lena. It could have been that she felt that this was her part of the bargain, that as a good guest she needed to be sociable. But it felt to Lena like more: talking with Win, she could feel some kind of ballast being released, as though Win needed to talk, and to her in particular, and she was surprised at how quickly they became intimate. Lena had many friends on Peliatos, and many of those were dearer to her than her own family, but in those cases it had taken years, not weeks, of contact. The evening that she told Win about Raleigh, they had sat and talked in her office for what ended up being three hours. She told Win everything, every detail of the day, and things she didn't tell the other islanders: that he had been drinking, not a lot but not a little, that she was going to keep him from going out but changed her mind, since it was going to be the last of the good weather. That they had fought, badly, the morning before he headed out. She spoke as Win sat dead quiet, telling her about the days that followed, the attempts to reconstruct, to understand, and how for a week the crews trolled the coast but never found his body. The calls to his parents once his parents were located, the memorial service, and then the slow sliding of the life of the island back into its everyday routines while she, alone, sat in their house above the trees and mourned.

Now, she is in a house full of people. Marcus, asleep on the couch, and Win and Ana in the room opposite hers. Lena opens the pill container with clumsy fingers, bending down slowly to drink from the tap, then sits with the leftovers of yesterday's coffee to wait for the day to begin.

CHAPTER NINE

KITT HAS LITTLE USE FOR HISTORY. IT IS something to be mined, at best. And in secret. He makes sure that stuff he lifts is untraceable—the last thing he'd want to be accused of is *homage*. Maybe this worked for other designers, but Kitt was bent on originality. So when he borrowed, which was often, he made sure to erase his tracks, and the irony of this never really hit him, was never allowed to settle; he moved too fast for that. So far no one had caught on. The language that he rallied around himself, that he used to frame each upcoming line, was the language of innovation, and the new summer line was this at its most emphatic. These were garments made of science, woven out of the future. The official phrasing. But, of course, behind all of that, obscured and cloaked so that no one but him and his few designers would see, was the source.

It's basically impossible for Kitt to think of anything other than the thing, the event, the fuck-all catastrophe that he knows is going to tank him, but he sits in his hotel room and goes through the material on his laptop in a kind of stupor anyway. There's little left to do, in terms of the launch; he'd set all of that up before he came here. He doesn't want to think about whether or not it's going to happen, whether the line will even see the light of day. Some part of him knows that if it does, it will only be after he steps down, after he's excised from the brand like a cancer. And to see the work, his best work, come out then, attributed to—who? Fucking Tomi and Nazim, probably. Who did pretty much nothing on this line, mostly because he was so obsessively protective of it, wouldn't really let anyone near it. So maybe this is what he deserved, in the end. What would he have wanted—to be killed off, and have the line survive, or to stay and have to scrap it all? He figured they'd offer him a silent partnership, but it's not the revenue he cares about. He has enough money for a long time, especially now that the charges have been dropped. Maybe enough to finish the building. If not, enough to liquidate, sell off the machinery, sell off the land, build somewhere else once things cool down. It's not like Peliatos was that unique, in the end. But he knows he doesn't have it in him, doesn't have the nerve to act in any way at all. Maybe he'll just move back to the city. His apartment's been kept clean, it's ready for him. He could get out of fashion, invest in a restaurant, a vineyard, or in something bigger—he could do what he does now but do it for industry, for government. He could come to the head of the big machine.

They wouldn't care about all of this. Maybe it would even count in his favour.

He's clicking through password-protected PDF files, pulling up invoices, scrolling along digital versions of the catalogue, the design briefs. Here's the history, the mood board, what gave Kitt the idea of the geometry of the pieces. This is more distracting than the other stuff so he sticks with it, looking back now at the invisible precedents, seeing how much made its way through. He can't remember whose work this was; he picked the images but the layouts aren't his. They're good. Hi-res scans of photographs gone *are-bure-boke* through reproduction and the shit tech of Soviet cameras and lithographs. Clippings from fashion magazines with names like *Rabotnitsa Moda* and *Siluett*. Clothes for workers, clothes for wives, clothes for functionaries—all these uncanny near-miss approximations of Britwave and Milanese trends, skewed and warped as they passed through the Iron Curtain. The best stuff is the early material, the heavy material, with the hangover of the severe fifties—all of those blocky shapes, the wide cuts with the hem up high and the sleeves coming way down past and ending in a thick cuff. This is the stuff that Kitt can really get into. What they did best was how the clothing seemed both totally abstracted yet utilitarian at the same time, how they'd index the rectangular cut of the workshirt with an oversized front pocket, singular, asymmetrical, though probably there was some purpose for this, too. For your brick of rationed cigarettes, maybe, or a pocketbook, or identification papers. It didn't matter, really. It was naïve, all of it, which made it better, and which made it easier to steal. The silhouettes are all wrong, or they were back then if you look at what everyone else was doing. They were just like the Soviet cars, all angles, no curves, even when a few nation-states over they were making Lamborghinis and Ferraris that looked like they were poured out of a tube. No tapering here, no tailoring; these clothes weren't meant to hug the body, but to reformat it, to turn an individual into an aggregate mass. Kitt's exact aesthetic. And to take these tendencies, and to finish them now, to render them in the proprietary fabric: ghosts will applaud. Though of course Kitt has no truck with communism—*I mean, look at what it's done to this place*—and maybe he even experiences a certain kind of perverse delight in taking the clothes of the proletariat and blasting them into the economic stratosphere. Into the future, out of the stupid past; from the factory to the storefront. In any case, the catwalk program practically wrote itself, but the trick was to only flirt with these references—no lockstep, no steely gaze, just the geometry of it and a subliminal kind of *déjà vu*. This was all he wanted from the source material, and after the launch he'd trash the files, burn the records, make everyone who worked on the project sign NDAs as thick as a phone book.

That is, of course, if it happened at all. If his life didn't end on this island, functionally speaking. If he fucked this up they'd just flip him overboard and go back to the old stuff, run off the templates instead; they'd reverse the past five years and go back to making wetsuits. He could probably sue them into dust if this happened, but who would want to represent him? There's probably a game to play here, a performance of atonement, contrition, et cetera. Maybe if he could do it right he'd come out of this, not on top, per se, but relatively unscathed. But none of his people are talking to him anymore, and even the qi gong guy has blown him off, which means he's operating on full tension with zero chemical assistance and feeling pretty fucking antagonistic, and if he tried to play the repentant role he'd probably fuck it up anyway. And with that, a knock on his door.

They're here now. Could he run? The suite only had one exit. The balcony was a thirty foot drop to harsh rock and surf. He could lock himself in the bathroom. He could refuse to open the door, though soon enough they'd bring someone from the hotel under the pretense of checking on him and gain entry anyway. There's nothing incriminating in here, aside from himself. The facts are pretty much all out *there*, in the end. There was nothing he could do, nothing he could say. The body was there. Or it was somewhere else now, sprayed clean, undressed, burnt to ash. Kitt feels like he's going to throw up, only all the time, now. They scattered the remains in the ocean, he can see the beach where they did it, he can feel it, smell it, in the air, or at least he thinks he can. He's having the interview at the hotel room because doing it at the site would be a PR nightmare of scrotal-tightening proportions. So, they're here. They're ringing his phone now, and knocking on his door at the same time. He can hear them calling his name. It will only get worse. So what can he do but close the laptop, stand up, walk to the door, and open it?

CHAPTER TEN

THE CLICK OF THE CAMERA'S SHUTTER IS inaudible now, hidden underneath the hungry noise of the tires on the road and the buffeting air coming through where the door used to be. Ana doesn't hear the mechanism at all until she comes to a stop to let a deer pass. The animal stares at her blankly, and she hears the click-click of the camera; some wildlife for the data-bank. It dashes off into the woods, and Ana brings the van back to speed. She's alone. Win stayed at the cabin, to do something in the garden with Lena. Ana's foam cuff is off for good, now, and she's trying to use her neck like she used to, but there's a strange resistance to the movements, like the brace is still on. The doctor said that her muscles and tendons would be shortened, shrunk by the pull of scar tissue. "Hungry," was the word he used—the scar tissue was hungry.

Early that morning, Ana had opened the back door of the van and crawled inside with the technology. Cables, loosened from their ceiling grommets, hung like vines, and the floor crunched with bits of broken plastic. She found the section of the hard-drive array that had come loose in the collision. It had snapped free of its bracket and, in its course towards the ground, pulled loose several of its neighbours, and these dangled by their coaxial wires but seemed otherwise intact. Ana went from each to each, carefully feeling them, searching for cracks. She'd have to see later if any of the lights still came on. The drive that lay on the bed of the van was totalled, its shell cracked open from the impact, and she pushed it to one side with her foot and set to removing it from the series. Technically speaking she should be able to bypass the broken drive, taking it out of the array, and she was sure that the remaining four would be more than enough storage for the rest of the job. But she couldn't remember which direction the drives were sequenced in—whether they filled up top-to-bottom, or bottom-to-top. She knew that the camera sent the images, as they were generated, in an alternating stream between two drives; this was the only way things could work, given the size of each high-resolution 360° panorama and the speed with which they were sent down from the camera. If one of those two drives was the one that obliterated itself in the crash, at worst they'd lose every other image, leaving the section of road striped with blank space every ten or so feet. Not a huge problem; they'd just edit the gaps out and offer the segment at a discount. Maybe the shattered drive was empty to begin with, and they lucked out.

Building computers in a computer factory—this is what her mother thought she was doing, what she went to university for. Some spectre of the old regime, in that image, but it wasn't like Gigi had lived that life herself. She was a teenager when the iron curtain was sprung, worked at a shopping mall in a suburb of Wroclaw, not in a munitions depot. She came to the new world out of caprice, more because she wanted to be far from her parents than because she wanted to give "a better life" to her own children. Gigi found a bubble of Polska in the new world, got a job in logistics working in the satellite office of an importer based out of Warsaw. She half-learned English, married, divorced, and leaned hard on her only child to go to school. No factories for her daughter, and no shopping malls, either. So Ana went to school, but not in business like she was told to. Instead: "building computers."

Ana traced the ends of the loose wires back to the array and then felt along the back of the rack-mounted server until she found where they plugged in. It was a quick switch, and in a few minutes she had everything wired back up. She kicked a clean patch out of the litter of plastic and wire and sat down. It was cool and dark inside the van, and just as damp with dew as the grass outside; all that meticulous weatherproofing and hermetic sealing made useless when Win's door caved in.

The camera was an entirely different situation. One of the tree's branches had clipped it as the van went careening off of the road, and now it was hanging off its mount at a drunken angle, held in place by a length of cable. It didn't look good. But who knew. The camera's spherical glass enclosure was inscrutable, an occulted all-seeing eye. If something was broken inside she wouldn't know until she was back in the depot downloading the files. Ana secured it back to the roof rack with half a roll of electrical tape and hoped for the best.

SHE DECIDED TO KEEP GOING, TO RECORD WHATEVER of the island she could before they left. They didn't ask her to, but they didn't specify otherwise, so here she is—business as usual, though there's plenty that's changed. She had snipped the bloodied air bags out of the dash with shears she borrowed from Lena's shed, scraped off as much of the leaf muck as she could from the windshield, and, with the help of Marcus, unbolted the smashed-in passenger-side door. Now, as she drives, the island comes through the open space, the air smelling of dense, wet evergreen, sharpened now and then by the pungent stink of skunk cabbage. Narrow driveways are scrolling past on her right side, and to the left, the same ridge of broken rock, interrupted here and there by narrow inlets leading to the interior roads. She picks one at random, cuts left, and enters the the tangled inner network of the island.

This all was pristine forest fifty years ago, but unlike the highway, the road Ana is on now wasn't carved out by industry. Swarms of hippie radicals came to the island in the dying years of the seventies, fleeing the cities that, whether through pricing or policing, pushed them out. They came and set up encampments, tarp cities that turned into settlements that turned into the mazy domestic interior of the island as it is today. The paths that criss-crossed between the nodes of the improvised commune, widened by heavy foot traffic, were ploughed into roads by the wheels of the cars that the new ferries could bring over—hippie cars, most likely, peeling Volvos and the ever-present Volkswagen bus, but cars nonetheless. If they wanted Peliatos to remain pristine, Ana thinks, they should have left the cars behind. But then, seemingly overnight, it was the eighties; during that decade of giddy growth, Peliatos was transformed by mainland capital interest from a neglected post-industrial island to a sought-after vacation spot. Its winding network of overgrown roads were tarmacked in a hurry, in order to convey not anarchists but athletic retirees. Or, really, a mixture of both, in a ratio that swung in and out of balance with the waxing and waning of the tourist season. The dropouts and go-getters, the hippies and yuppies, everyone pushing seventy, eighty—same generation, same impulse to rebel, just followed through different channels. Ana wasn't sure how different the two were, if one took the long view; in any case it all seemed antique to her. She had a hard time feeling any kind of connection to the generation above hers. She was twenty-eight and dealing with her own shit, her own zeitgeist. The cracked and weathered pavement under the van's tires was so ancient that it didn't look or feel much different from the island's igneous rock. Ana feels like an equalizing force: camera firing away, mapping out whatever dark corners were left, reconciling all of that historical baggage—smoothing and reformatting, ironing out the folds and ripples.

Ana notices something new about the island's nomen-
clature on today's drive. There are the expected touches
of local character, with streets named after resident flora
and fauna, as well as a handful that accord to different
stages of Buddhist enlightenment. But many of the roads
on Peliatos share names with those on the mainland, as
if something—prior waterways, trade thoroughfares,
pre-tectonic alignments—once connected them together.
Back on the ferry, she had noticed that the path the vessel
was taking was limned on her phone's map as if it were a
continuation of the highway; now, as she learned, dozens
of these connections held invisibly, the coastal arteries
resuming on the little blip of land as if there were no gap
in between. These must have predated the hippies, must
have resulted from a kind of nostalgia on the part of the
island's industrial-era settlers, if not simply from a lack of
imagination. Little bits of the sworn-off home, metropol-
itan streets preserved in miniature in the middle of the
forest.

Ana keeps expecting to pass a street sign from her
childhood, but a few minutes into the tangle of roads she's
too engrossed by the maze to even notice if she did. Half of
the roads are hardly longer than a van-length, pinging off
in acute angles and curving back to each other, branching
and twinning erratically in an illogical spiderweb. It's the
neurotic opposite of the rationalized city plan, following
no pattern—or, following a pattern, but an obscure one,
and one buried by the passage of years, all the layers of
new usage falling like deadwood over the original paths. It
must still have made sense to someone, one of the island's

many aging longhairs, one of the ones who walked the old network connecting caravans, campers, cabins; but it's alien to Ana. She rounds a corner in the van and comes across the same moss-covered shed again, and finally has to admit that she's lost. She gets out of the van and looks around. She's still unwilling to check her phone, is convinced that if she works hard enough she can assemble the map in her head; so she just stands, leaning against the front of the van, camera clicking, until someone comes out from one of the houses.

It's an older man who looks exactly like what Ana imagined all the islanders look like—grey hair, grey beard, a ratty old sweater, and an aura of something between naiveté and aloofness. He walks down the drive, making irregular use out of a wooden walking stick, and asks her if she needs help. She says no, and he asks if she's sure. She says yes. He pauses for a minute, looks at the van, and then asks her if she'd like to come in for a cup of coffee. Without knowing why, she says, yeah, okay, and she follows him as he turns around and heads back indoors. The camera is still clicking, which means that if she's murdered, there will at least be evidence.

His cabin is a collage of different materials—weather-bleached cedar shingles, broad sections of painted chip-board, and screwed-on sheets of corrugated metal—all organized together slapdash over what seems like many, many years of use. To get to it they walk past a camper van whose custard-yellow body is streaked with mildew, its tires baggy and cracked. A dog pops out from somewhere to sniff at Ana's ankles.

Inside is dark, and muggy with the weight of wood and shag. Another dog, an old hound grown arthritic and barrel-bodied, lies on its side next to the fireplace. The crackling of the fire eating the logs, and the sound of a coffee maker burbling in the kitchen. Ana sits down on a plaid couch with the thought, a thought she has often, that she wishes she could just *ctrl-Z* undo the last couple of decisions that brought her here, but of course now it's too late. The man comes back into the room with a tray: mugs, creamer, sugar, some cookies that Ana doesn't even have to see to know she won't touch. He puts it down on the side table and sits down across from her, which means that conversation is about to start.

Ana is not a conversationalist. She is not the kind of person to strike up a chat with a stranger, or to sustain one that has been started by someone else. Her conversational style is to listen, less out of interest than out of a kind of option-paralysis, an inability to commit to any particular speech act. Not from over-investment, or even anxiety, but from the opposite—from a deep sense that each and every response or utterance is equally flat, equally without any intrinsic value outside of its use as a kind of currency. So who cares? Why bother? When she watches other people talk, in all of their animation and exchange, she feels like a zoologist watching the intercourse of animals. Birds who pass the same fish back and forth, beak to beak, over and over. If you stop believing in the fish, the whole thing falls apart, and Ana isn't sure that she ever believed in the fish. So when the man begins to speak, Ana's brain does the thing it always does—it splits off into a host of processes and sub-processes, each spinning out its various programs in the infinitesimal gaps between words and sense. She tries to calculate the right response, but the problem is that the words keep coming. Particularly from this individual.

After the formality of names—his name is Finlay, her name is Ana—he asks her what brings her to the island, but it's clear from his demeanour that he knows. The van doesn't exactly fit in, and she, as an extension of it, is similarly marked. She might as well have a camera on her head. She tells him she's here for work; he asks what work. The coffee gives her a reason to pause, and she exploits that—the coffee, hot and dark like a headache, in a mug that was once from a diner called Susanne's. She says "surveying." It's either too vague or not vague enough because he presses on.

"Surveying, what kind? Do you work for the municipality?"

"No. Private." Ana thinks: what is the trick with tone, the thing that ends the line of questioning?

"Ah. I think I know what you mean."

"Do you?" Part of it, she thinks, is not answering a statement with a question, but answering a statement with another statement. A shorter statement, as short as possible. So she's messed that up.

"The developments, the rezoning, the resorts. What's next, I wonder. Casinos. A highway across the water. McDonalds."

"I don't know."

"You don't know, or you don't want to say?"

"My role in this is—minimal."

"You're here, aren't you?" Is this threat in his tone? No, it's inquisitiveness. Nosiness. Or is it nothing, just banter, just making conversation.

"I'm here. Working. They sent me over to take pictures."

"Spec-ops. I get it. You're the forerunner."

"Of a sort."

"You're the one who comes first."

"First before what?"

"You know what."

"Sure. I'm here, and then other people come and they build new buildings, tear down old ones." Statements, statements. He's trying to get her to tell him what she thinks he knows so that he can know it.

"Exactly. I can read you out a list, from memory."

"Of what?"

"Look at your cup." She looks down: Suzanne's, in red script. "You know where that was?"

"Where."

"Under the resort. So was the surf shop, the original one. And Heron Books. And the old greenmarket, before they had to shove it into the back of the corner store. Sacha's Paint and Art Supply. Squashed flat. Scraped into bins and taken to the dump."

"Minus this cup," Ana says.

"Minus that cup. And whatever else we could salvage before it was all carted off."

"So I am supposing you're not a fan of the resort."

"I couldn't afford to be, if I wanted to. I worked at Heron."

"And now?"

"And now what."

"And now where do you work?"

"Employment insurance. When that runs out, I start selling things off. Records. Books. Stuff from the shed."

"Why not work somewhere on the island?"

"No jobs. This thing happens when you knock out a whole block of shops and restaurants and put one big resort on top of it. The thing being that suddenly there are no jobs."

"Why not work at the resort?"

"You really think that anyone from the island works at Windermere?"

"I honestly never thought about it."

"Of course you didn't. Why would you?"

"I assumed they'd have to hire from people who lived here."

"As if. The only local jobs the resort brought with it were laughable. The kid of a friend of mine applied for a reception and bookings gig, turned out it was an unpaid internship. The only benefit we got from Windermere was, they had to throw some money our way—improve some of the roads, put an addition on our hospital, but that was mostly just in case a wealthy hiker slipped and fractured their skull."

"Oh."

"We didn't have anything they wanted. Peliatos doesn't exactly produce five-star chefs and Swedish massage therapists."

"Maybe it should?"

"I can't even start with explaining why it shouldn't, or couldn't."

Ana redirects her attention to the coffee. She has less of an urge to get out of there than before, but if she finishes the coffee it will give her an ending that she can deploy when she needs to, an escape in reserve. As in, she thanks him for the coffee and then she leaves. And she can do this at any point, starting now, and knowing this gives her a bit of unexpected torque, quickens her into a new frame of relation.

"Can I ask you something?" He makes a sound of assent. "What was there before?"

"Before the resort?"

"No, before the surf shop, the bookstore. What did those replace?"

"Ah. It was, I think, the same buildings but different stores. Maybe there was a community association in what turned into the surf shop."

"And before that?"

"I don't know."

"For any of them?"

"Heron Books was built by the owner."

"So what was there before?"

"There was nothing there before."

"Nothing? A void? A vacuum?"

"I think there was some kind of shed before. Noel built an extension on it, turned it into the bookstore."

"And before that?" Ana has an end in mind but she could also keep doing this a while longer, just to see the man taken off his guard like this. He's sitting back in his chair, as though physically restrained. Ana doesn't think she's ever been able to do something like this before.

"I guess you could say, forest. Or maybe a clearing. I don't know, it was forever ago."

"Okay."

"Okay?"

"You can see how, from my perspective, this might seem ..."

"I really don't know what you're talking about." He looks perplexed; this she can read.

"What comes after the resort?"

"Oh, I get it. Cynical, cynical. City mindset. The endless cycle. You've talked me into something, here."

"I've communicated my view."

"Which is?"

"That the resort knocking down your bookstore isn't different from your bookstore knocking down that shed." This puts a pause in the conversation, during which Finlay refills both of their coffee cups.

"There's a difference you wouldn't get," he says.

"Sentimental?"

"Sure. Put it that way."

"It is sentimental to not accept change—or that's what people say."

"But not all change is good."

"By your logic, all change is bad."

"Maybe it is? If you want to really—if you get down to the base of it, it's all bad, even the shed." He seems to be settling into something, shifting.

"I think you could even say, *especially* the shed. The shed had no right to be there, right? But once it was, the bookstore, the resort, those made sense."

"I remember now an important detail. There was another building. A pub. Where the resort is now. The only one on the island, at least back then."

"What happened to it? Did they knock it down to build the shed?"

"No. There was an earthquake, a small one. Really more of a landslide. But the pub was too close to the shore and it was ruined."

"It fell in?"

"Its foundations gave way. The shale loosened, it wasn't built well enough. It would have been too difficult to fix so they just tore it down."

"And then they built a shed?"

"It could have been that the shed was attached to it, and that after the accident it was all that's left. Or maybe the shed was nowhere near it. Have you seen the Windermere? It's gigantic. It covers that whole end of the island."

"And you're just remembering it now?"

"I didn't forget the earthquake, just that the shed was involved."

"Which I suppose it wasn't."

"Thankfully. That became the bookstore."

"Does this sort of thing happen often? Earthquakes?"

"Well you've heard of the horror stories. The 'Big One.' But no, not really. Here and there. We have more issues with fires than with earthquakes, if you'll believe that. And even with all this rain."

"What are we talking about, here? Forest fires?"

"No, not that. Nothing will catch in the forests, it's all waterlogged year-round. In the village. Electrical problems. The old wiring wasn't good—the buildings were pretty much thrown together. By people like me. Not to code. And then even some of the newer buildings, I don't know why. Probably the whole system is compromised."

"So you have earthquakes, you have fires. Do you have floods?"

"We've had a couple. Mostly when we've had an unseasonably cold winter, and then the spring melt. Depends where you are. Nothing extreme. Most people here are more likely to drown in the ocean."

"And this ... happens?"

"I'm not trying to scare you off. But, yes. Too often. Usually surfers. Sometimes fishermen. Swimmers. There are powerful currents, if you're not careful. People get sucked out into the channel. We end up calling the Coast Guard a few times every summer. Some people go off of the cliffs. Some on purpose, but even that can end badly. Especially that."

"Can you give me some sense of death count here."

"For your survey?"

"Sure."

"It's—I'm aware of how this sounds. It's high."

"How high is high?"

"Last summer, five people. Six."

"Can't you put up signs? Fences? Get lifeguards?"

"We have all these things. You can't even take a surfboard out without getting a permit."

"I've seen the waves."

"People come out here for it. Sometimes it's too much for them, I guess."

"So you have property damage, floods, drownings, fires."

"When you put it that way."

"And a person killed by concrete."

"You want to know something? What it seems like to me?"

"Okay."

"Sometimes it seems like the island—I'm a rational person. I don't go in for this stuff like other people do here. But sometimes it seems like the island wants us off of it."

"Off of it?"

"I understand entropy, and chaos, but there's always a part of me that, when I hear about the latest thing, I think, 'yes, well.' Not a flattering thing to say, I know. Not very neighbourly. I do love it here. I love Peliatos. It's been my home for forty years. But then again, you have to ask, sometimes—what are we *doing* here?"

AFTER THE COFFEE IS FINISHED, ANA THANKS HIM and heads out. He walks her back to the van, to which he gives a longer look—the dents, the broken mirrors, the taped-up camera. She climbs up into the driver's seat and closes the door. He taps her window, and when she rolls it down he asks her, again, whether she needs help with directions. Ana looks at him and shakes her head in a stiff left-right, meaning, *no thanks* and *no thanks for asking*. She waves goodbye, and then starts the van and drives through to the next fork in the road, then the next, and the next. It's not until a while later, when she's found her way out of the maze and is driving back to Lena's, that she recognizes that gesture, a micro-gesture, almost, retracted and stubborn, as her mother's. This is not a comparison that Ana leans into.

The van covers the road, the camera firing, as the light comes through the breaks in the trees or is blocked by the heavy branches. With each click, the picture, or the nothing at all, comes skimming down the cables at the speed of light and embeds itself in the hard drives—first one, then the other, and then back again, each image broken into zeroes and ones and intermixed with itself.

CHAPTER ELEVEN

THE SPOT THE FAMILY PICKED IS, OF COURSE, by the ocean. It's a wet morning, with the tide far out and the rocky cove scattered with coils of glossy kelp. In the centre of the crescent-shaped beach, someone had started a kind of shrine, had put down a blanket and on top of that some candles and a framed photograph, and as the crowd gathered more photos, and more candles, were added, the photographs ranging from large framed pictures of the girl to little polaroids and wallet-sized portraits that looked like they were from high school. The candles flicker against the drizzle, and are constantly going out, and someone is always bending over with a barbecue lighter to get one started again, but Win thinks that it is beautiful anyway—all of that candlelight flickering on the beach.

They scattered the remains a few days ago, a private thing with just Marcus and his mom and some friends. Win can barely even think about that, how that must have felt. And now, today, is the public event. Lena went to both, but Win and Ana obviously were not invited to the first one, nor is Win sure she could have handled herself if she did. Her threshold for this kind of thing is very, very low, and she feels hyper-attuned to the emotions around her. There's a feeling in the air of a pretty forced, well, celebration, as in "celebration of life"; Win's been to some funerals, but this is the first she's gone to like this. When a grandparent dies you're sad but you're ready for it, or at least that's what it seemed like for her, even when she was a teenager, but what could possibly prepare you for this? She was so, so young, and to have it happen like that, and everyone seeing it—those images are hanging in everyone's heads, competing against all of these sweet photographs. The dead grey hand.

It's early enough that the beach is mostly empty, and the three of them, Win, Ana, and Lena, go for a walk away from the rest of the mourners. Win and Ana are the only ones here who didn't know the girl, and it seems, the only ones who don't know everyone else, but people know them. They're minor celebrities: the ones who crashed into Lena's house, the weird ones from away, the ones with the camera van. This last detail generates some hostility, which Win understands—who wants to be spied on?—but it's about more than just privacy. They understand what Win and Ana being on the island means, what the significance of the van and its roadside documentation is. Being under Lena's wing has done a lot to ingratiate them with the islanders, but they're still, if not the enemy, then at least in cahoots with the enemy: they're the vanguard of change, and it's a deeply unwanted change. A destruction, is what it is, and the more time Win spends with Lena and her friends, the more she wants to smash the van's camera with a hammer. She supposes that the crash probably did that for them. Win has no problems with taking part in the flipping of dead ex-industrial lots, with the revitalization of abandoned landscapes, but this seems different in a number of pretty important ways. She's been chewed out by Marcus about all of this, in an lengthy conversational crusade he launched against her the first night, over dinner, and if she indulged his ranting, it was only in part because she knew it was distracting him from other matters. She knew the problems with what they were doing. It was pretty simple. There just wasn't that much room left on Peliatos; even the cliffs had quirky shacks climbing up them. Everything that wasn't national parkland was someone's home and in order for the future to come to Peliatos, it was going to have to displace a whole lot of the past. And that was them, the future: Win and Ana, but also, she realized, Kitt, too, all wrapped up in this too-big thing together.

Win looks back at the crowd, larger now. She wonders if Kitt is in there, whether he came to pay his respects, or if he was too afraid of what would happen if he showed. He was still on the island, holed up in his top-tier room in the resort, and god knows why. If it was her, she would have fled the island on the first ferry out and left these people alone. Maybe he thinks he's doing some kind of penance. Penance with room service.

Someone separates themself from the group and begins to speak, so the three of them make their way back—Ana and Lena on either side of Win, arms around her, so she doesn't slip on the rocks.

It's Marcus, giving the speech, with someone beside him who must be his mother. Based on her appearance, she took the ferry in. How much did she know about the lives of her children, her Marcus and Stephanie hidden away on this dark little island? Was she in touch? It didn't occur to Win that Marcus would have parents, that there'd be other people involved in this aside from him, but there she is—Mrs. Farwell, looking sort of, the word was "posh," and very out-of-place surrounded by hippies on the muggy beach. Marcus's speech is moving but is full of references that Win doesn't understand, islandisms and fragments of stories from his sister's life on Peliatos. Stephanie worked at the island's one café and otherwise, you got it, surfed. She moved here first, before Marcus; she is why he came over in the first place. She loved Peliatos. She was planning a trip to Australia for the spring. She was twenty-two. Win listens to Marcus speak, and then his mother says a few things, and then the two of them rejoin the crowd or, more like, the crowd rejoins them, everyone coming forward and enveloping mother and son in a sort of collective embrace.

A guitar is brought out, and the gathering takes on a more informal tone. Win smells a few different kinds of smoke. Ana and Lena drift off somewhere, leaving Win alone, and she walks through the mourners to the little shrine, still flickering away. The glass fronts of the picture frames are fogged and the jars of the candles are filling with water. Win bends down and picks up one of the pictures, wiping the dew or mist off of it with her sleeve. It's a picture of Stephanie and Marcus, looking sci-fi in their wetsuits, a hazy Fujifilm beach in the background. Stephanie is taller than her brother, and has her arm around his shoulders. Her face is tanned and sunglass-stencilled, her eyes, a blue that is startling even in the cheap photo print, are crinkled with a goofy surfer-stoner grin. Win looks at the photo for a minute and then bursts into a total mess of facial waterworks.

There's no real end to the memorial; people hang around all morning and into the afternoon, as sun gradually burns off the fog and the green-grey water goes a few shades lighter. Win, Ana, and Lena stay until the tide has come in, and help Marcus and his friends move the blanket and photographs and candles to higher ground. They leave the group sitting on the grass and the three of them head to the truck, parked on a side road nearby. They make the short trip back to Lena's, no one speaking, and pull in next to the battered van in the driveway. Ana opens Win's door for her, and she grabs her crutch and slides out. The bottom of Win's cast is soggy, and her toes sticking out are grey with muck; she'd have put a plastic bag around it if there were any on the island, which, of course, there aren't.

CHAPTER TWELVE

THE TRUCK PULLS OUT OF THE PARKING LOT and back onto the road, Win waving out of the passenger window. They've dropped Ana off on the way back from the memorial; she told them she had to get something for the van but mostly right now she just feels a deep need for space. There's a kind of fuse that starts going in Ana's head whenever she's in that genre of high-intensity social environment, something that counts down towards zero, towards being alone again. And that, the funeral, memorial, celebration, whatever, was without a doubt the most intense thing she's had to do. She's never had less control over her entrances and exits than she's had on this island, and this afternoon felt like that feeling's apex. All of those people, all of that intimacy, and her and Win on the outside of it—Ana's not sure why they went and wouldn't have if Win didn't want to, and there were moments when Win and Lena went off somewhere and left Ana by herself to be accosted by someone or other with that question, the *how did you know her*, which of course Ana had to answer, that she didn't, that she didn't know any of them, and after that the conversation gets pretty weird and pretty short.

The door of the hardware store clinks shut with a nautical wind chime of shells and seaglass; the storekeeper looks up from his inventory to offer an overly enthusiastic salutation. Ana wants to jump into a city like a person on fire wants to jump into a lake. She lacks the inner mechanics to get into Peliatos the way that Win has—friendly, flexible, foodie Win, at home anywhere. There aren't enough people here to make a crowd to get lost in. She's had to improvise. While Win's been looking into mushroom foraging, Ana has spent the past three days elbow deep in the guts of the van. It doesn't feel like she's avoiding everyone, but that's probably what it is. Her latest project is tending to the battered camera, replacing the ad hoc mount with something more durable than tape. The lens, at least, seemed intact; the damage was localized, purely infrastructural, a matter of brackets, supports, pins and receptacles. Not unlike Win's leg, but this at least Ana could fix.

She's on an exploratory mission here in this tiny lean-to of a hardware store, looking for material to repurpose. If she were repairing a shingled roof, or painting a chicken coop, or building a gazebo, she'd have an easier time of it; she's hungry for plastic in a wooden world. She settles for some aluminum gate hinges and a coil of wire, and wanders down the power tool aisle in search of something aggressive. The impact drill is just sitting out, not chained to the counter, and it feels good in her hand, all that battery and motor weight. She lifts it up like a high-bore revolver and is aiming it down the aisle, clicking the trigger, when Kitt walks into her sights.

He pauses for a beat, then keeps walking towards her. Ana pulls the trigger a few more times as he approaches and then puts the drill back on the shelf. He looks better than he did on TV, like he's showered and shaved and maybe gone to the gym. Ana has no idea why he's still here. Well, she has an idea. She supposes he's here for the same reason she's here, inertia; he can't possibly expect to finish building his house, or at least not for a while. Why is he in the hardware store, then? But again, why is *she*. Maybe he's also tinkering with ruins.

Kitt stands next to her and looks at the display. Ana takes a packaged drill from the shelf and drops it into her shopping cart. She can feel his scrutiny, can feel the tension of his presence. She has no idea what she's expected to say to him, but knows she should say something.

She turns to him, and says, *I killed someone, too.*

CHAPTER THIRTEEN

I T'S ONLY FOUR O'CLOCK BUT IT'S ALREADY DARK inside Lena's house, the sun choked out by the trees all around. Always the trees. Win couldn't understand how Lena could grow anything in this perpetual shade, but her garden was thriving, somehow. Ana goes around turning on lights, and then joins Win on the couch in front of the beach window. It's the same view as at the memorial: the ocean, the fog now pulled back, blurring the line between horizon and sky. The beach is different, though, with its brilliant shells instead of wet black rocks. Lena's bit of coast is beautiful, the only of its kind Win's seen anywhere on the island. In the patches of sunlight the shells sparkle like crushed china, like a million bits of shredded tin. The waves, leading the way for the tide, shuffle and reshuffle the pieces.

Ana is back from the hardware store, empty-handed.

She has her legs up on the couch, feet up against Win, and with her foam cuff off, she looks completely normal—or as normal as Ana gets, her face underlit from the laptop screen and the supersized phone she's holding up between that screen and her eyeballs. And then there's Win, her leg, the plaster gone way off-white with all of the Pacific Northwest detritus that's stuck to it over the past weeks, even, she notices now, some cooking oil. Another month before it comes off. By that time, she assumes, she'll be back home. Win has stopped feeling for an end point, has been caught up in all of what's been happening, but knows that eventually the two of them will pack up, get on the ferry, and get themselves home. Home to their dead houseplants and rotting fridges and overflowing mailboxes. Home to whatever the next scrubbing job is, back to her nine-to-five, or noon-to-eight-or-midnight; back to the ordinary. Back to probably no more away jobs for a while.

Win gives Ana's foot a little squish and then slumps down low in the couch, looking out the window. It must be a strong tide—the waves are coming in faster and harder than Win has seen them, their tops splintered into wavelets and dashed with foam. The water has darkened, gone a deep glassy grey, and the branches of the white pines that dip down into the top of the window's frame are thrashing in a hard wind. The sun's taken on a different aspect, too, a weird kind of haze hanging over it that the wind isn't pulling off. She can hear the underripe cones bouncing off of the roof's wooden shingles, like the sound that massive, golf-ball sized hail makes on a car windshield—they come rattling down one by one at first, and then faster, in percussive bursts that thicken until it's one big rolling noise. Lena comes in from the hall and looks out the window, then walks through to the kitchen. The waves are coming in hard now, crashing against the beach so loudly that Win can hear from the living room the heave of the water pulling back in, grey and full of shell matter. And the wind, too, carving around the cabin, thrumming along the washboard-slats of the exterior walls. Through the tines of the trees, the wind has an almost human voice, a kind of wild moan or howl, like something alive and in pain.

It's all building to a crescendo—the waves, the wind, the hammering of the pine cones—and it's loud enough that Ana looks up, and as her eyes meet Win's there's a violent shriek as a patch of shingles tears loose from the roof, and Win actually sees them, the shingles, carried by the wind *back towards the water*, which is weird—and then everything at all once goes quiet.

A few minutes pass. Lena is in front of the window, with her hands against the glass, looking out. No one says anything, and it's eerie, dead silent, with the sky all torn into purple and grey shreds, and not a trace of wind. Whatever it was, is over. Another meteorological event for the archives, Win figures, another bit of data to be analyzed by the computers in the shed.

Lena is turning away from the window when her phone starts ringing. And then the phone in Ana's hand starts ringing, too, and Win's phone in the other room, and finally, the landline joins in, its shrill alarm coming from right behind Win's head. Win turns around to pick it up in a weird half-thought reflex and before she's grabbed it,

Lena is calling to her from the centre of the living room, her eyes wide and her hands outstretched to both of them. Win grabs her crutch and struggles to her feet, Ana shaking off the laptop beside her, and Lena grabs hold of them and shouts over the din.

"We don't have much time. You need to get in the van. Ana, do you know how to get to the top of the ridge?" Ana nods yes. "There is a safe place there. I will meet you on the main road, Ponderosa, it is called, and show you the way. I have to go, I need to call it in. I have the emergency kits. I will meet you there. Pick up anyone that you see on the road. Anyone you see who needs help. Good?"

Win and Ana stumble out of the cabin. They're halfway to the van when the first siren starts, long and low and apocalyptic, and the sound of it sends Win into a deep, practically animal state of unease. She's jackhammering the crutch into the gravel, trying to take as much weight as she can on her good leg, and Ana is beside her, pulling her along. The van is parked on the street at the end of the drive, and its interior is littered with leaves that the wind carried through the doorless passenger side. The first siren is answered by another, this one much closer, and under the ear-splitting wail the two of them climb in and fire the ignition. Ana kicks out the emergency brake and pulls them onto the road. With the two sirens deadly loud and strobing in and out of phase, Win has to yell to be heard.

"Should we empty out the back? How much room do we have?"

"Not very much."

"And you know where we're going?"

"Yes," Ana says.

They're a few hundred feet down the road towards the southernmost point of the island when they spot their first passenger, a dark figure running with his back to them along the shoulder of the road. As they pull up beside him they slow to match his pace. It's Kitt Feldt, his eyes bugging out under the pulled-down hood of his jacket.

"What are you *doing*?" Win shouts at him from her seat.

"I thought I'd go for a fucking walk," Kitt says. "I didn't know the fucking world was about to end. What the fuck is happening?"

"Get in the van. The back is open." He does as told and climbs in through the double doors, bent over and feeling his way along the server racks. As soon as he's sat down on the floor of the van Ana hits the accelerator hard and they lurch back into the lane. They round the bend at the bottom of the island, passing the resort. When they pull over at the ferry terminal it's nearly deserted, thank god, with only a few bewildered tourists standing around. Kitt opens the doors and they climb inside. A car tears down the road towards them, between the two lanes, its driver holding down the horn and the note bending in pitch as it passes. In the back of the van the tourists confer in frantic German. There are felled branches all over the pavement, some thick enough that the van's suspension pops when they go over them, and the houses along the road look like they've been knocked around by a giant, like they've been shaken up in a wooded snowglobe. There are no more people on the road, not even other cars, and Win is hoping that everyone knew what the alarms meant and got to safety. But what did the alarms mean? Is it really happening, right now? She can't hold onto the thought against the blare of the sirens, still rising and falling, the rush of air through the opening, the vehicle and human noise coming from the back of the van. They take a side road and are on an incline, now, climbing fast; they're going up the ridge in the centre of the island. The engine is straining like crazy, it feels like it's going to give out any minute, and the road keeps getting steeper. Win can feel the elevation gain in her ears. She can't see anything, though, not past the thick cover of trees. There's a three-way pass in the road, and Ana turns left without slowing down—*Ponderosa Drive.* The ground begins to level out.

Kitt emerges from between the two seats and looks out of the windshield with them.

"Will it be safe up here?"

"That's what Lena says. Maybe we'll be high enough up. Look."

They see cars, old ratty Toyotas and pickup trucks and camper vans, parked along the road. The whole town, it seems like, but the vehicles are all empty, abandoned, their passengers having moved on. They drive until they see Lena's truck, stopped in the middle of the road. She's sitting on the tailgate, and the back of the pickup is full of people, teenagers, mostly, hunkered down among the duffle bags and crates. When she sees them she drops onto the pavement and, with a wave of her arm, climbs into the truck and starts the engine. They follow her, the kids in the pickup's box throwing bewildered looks back at them and their beat-to-hell van.

The sirens are faint now, down below, and the trees are starting to clear out. The sky is still bruise-purple, and the ocean, when Win can see it, is diced up into whitecaps. It's been five, maybe ten minutes. What was the lead time for the alarms? Lena's truck turns off onto a sloping, unpaved road, and they follow her. And here they all are, the island-ers, from their cars, walking up the steep double-track on the way to the shelter—lone walkers struggling under massive appliance-dangling packs, surfers in wetsuits loping along, mothers and fathers carrying infants, wild-haired hippie kids who run amok, either ignorant of what's happening or careless of it, raised with this scenario always somewhere in their heads. Everything is clattering around in the back of the van, and the pickup ahead of them is bucking and jolting and kicking up dust. Win's not sure how much time they have before whatever seismic or tectonic event, whatever it is, reaches them, but she hopes it's enough for everyone to get high, high up. And she hopes that way up here is high enough.

The road bends upon itself in an off-camber hairpin and lets out into a clearing. As Ana pulls the van beside Lena's truck the view fills their windshield and it's enough to make Win forget, for a second, why they're here. They're on a broad plateau, the top of the ridge, and below them the view goes on and on, all the way onto the Pacific, wide and violent and infinite, stretching out from the ragged edge of the island, and between it and them is the spread of Peliatos, the nude patches of settlement cut out of the green expanse, the highway a thin snaking cut, a finger-width groove etched into the thick mass of forest.

Ana hops out of the van and opens the back doors. The teenagers are taking the supplies out of Lena's truck and carrying them to the shelter—which is nothing like the bunker Win imagined, but instead a wooden cabin, an old A-frame deal with a wraparound deck that sticks way out over the cliff face. As she gets down from the van, Lena comes over to her.

"What do we do now?"

"All we can do is wait. The sensors were triggered, which means that something has happened, out there—I can't say what it is. If we're lucky, a minor earthquake."

"And if we're unlucky …"

"I've gone over the data. It's not clear. We'll know in ten, fifteen minutes."

"We'll know? You mean, like, when the wave comes and takes us all out?"

"We're not going to know until it happens, and we've done all we can."

"When was the last time—*this* happened? The alarms and everything?"

"The last time was ten years ago. I didn't have the alarm set up then. There wasn't the technology. We were up here when it happened, Raleigh and me."

"And what happened?"

"It was a minor earthquake."

"Did it look like this?"

"No."

Ana comes up, with Kitt and the tourists, and Lena directs them towards the cabin. The plateau is packed, now, and little camps have formed—clusters of families, their belongings or emergency kits or whatever else they brought with them piled up. People walk through the crowd, calling names. Someone has a cooler full of water bottles. It's like a big picnic—everyone seems pretty prepared, and while there's a definite tension in the air no one is freaking out. Maybe they think this is just another little shake-up. Maybe it is, or maybe it isn't. Win passes a group of adolescents who are, incomprehensibly, decked out in what looks like wizarding attire—pointed hats, flowing sleeves, wands, the works. One of them has a cape with THE DEFENDERS bedazzled onto it. There are babies playing in the mud, like in photographs of Woodstock, and wealthy vacationers standing around looking unsure and disassociated. Chefs still in their aprons, and old hippies with driftwood walking sticks. Every island archetype is crammed onto this tiny wedge of rock, and it is too much, too many people, way more than can possibly fit. The air is heavy and close and the clearing is crammed with bodies. Suddenly there's no space around her. She loses Ana and Kitt in the crowd, and almost has her crutch kicked out from under her, and can't see the cabin anymore. She stops and feels her phone vibrating, pulls it out, and it's another alarm.

Ana is suddenly next to her, lifting up Win's arm and putting it over her shoulder. They walk along together, the crowd parting in front of them. Win sees Marcus's face, for a second, and then he's gone, and they're at the cabin, sitting on a picnic bench on the deck.

"There was another one," Win says.

"I know." Ana's hair is pasted to her forehead with sweat.

"Do you think everyone else knows, too?"

"It doesn't seem like it."

"What does it mean, two alarms? Another quake?"

"I don't know. I guess."

"Shit, Ana—is this it?"

"I don't know. I don't know. I'm scared. I'm so scared and *why* are we *here*."

LENA COMES OUT OF THE CABIN, HEADING FOR THE mass of people, but Win grabs her arm as she passes. She turns and her face is set, mask-like. Win lets go and she jogs off and disappears into the crowd. Win doesn't know whether they should go inside, or stay where they are, or lie down on the ground. The weather is changing again— they're exposed, this high up, above the fringe of trees, and the wind is growing sharp and cold and full of plant- matter. There's moisture in the air, but it's not rain, or doesn't feel like the rain Win knows, coming at them hor- izontally, with a smell of the ocean and ozone. The freez- ing gusts of wind are cutting through her clothing and stinging her face, full of droplets right on the edge of hail. In between the gusts, in the momentary silence, Win can hear the sirens still, the two wailing tones going in and out of sync, and she knows that by now it's too late for anyone who is still down there, and she tries to think of what's happening on the mainland, what people are doing in the cities, if they know, or if the crowd huddled on the ridge were the only ones who know what was coming. Should she call? Who would she call? There's a cry from somewhere on the ridge, and everyone turns to face the ocean. Ana grabs Win and pulls her to her feet, and the two clutch each other and look out.

IT'S ALREADY COMING IN THE SHALLOWS WHEN SHE sees it, the water, crawling in from the depths towards the edge of the island, towards the beach, towards them. It's a deep, frothing wall, not a wave, or at least not like the waves Win has seen. It looks like a tall, humped slab of concrete, like liquid roadworks, mud-grey and angry. When it hits the island, Win can't feel it, but she can hear it, the concussion of all that weight against the shore. The edges of the wall get caught in the rocks, shattered into twenty- or thirty-foot high sprays of foam, but what is left is sharpened by the curvature of the cove into something angrier, more particular, a wedge that funnels hungrily inland. The sound the wave makes as it hits the houses along the beach—as it moves somehow right through them, like they were porous, a sieve—and then gathers up the bits into a sludge-brown slurry and moves onwards, crossing the road and digging into the forest somehow without losing an fraction of speed, the sound is primordial and cataclysmic. The trees give way, their tops sucked under, the splinters and spines forming a prickly froth that is pushed out to the edges of the boiling and churning wave. She sees a sailboat, riding on the tail of the rush for an instant and then flipping over, coming back up without a mast, and she feels like she's going to be sick, and the bubbling, roiling dagger of whitewater is moving quiet, now, or not fully quiet, but Win can hear everyone on the plateau screaming. Ana's nails are digging into her neck, and Win holds her closer, but neither of them turn towards each other. They can't look away, even though it's horrible, even though it's pure evil, the wave, or whatever you would call it now, bloated and fat from wreckage but still coming in. A second, two seconds, and it's almost upon them. It's rougher and wilder now, torn up by the rocks and the trees, losing some of its momentum as it tracks up the incline, as it comes straight at them like it knew where they were hiding. The leading edge churns up the sloping base of the cliff, and vanishes, which means that it is now underneath them, going vertical, the cabin and the deck shaking, the water roaring, and then it's everywhere, absorbing them entirely in an explosion of grey-green foam.

CHAPTER FOURTEEN

WIN IS RETCHING UP SEAWATER, HER sinuses burning with salt. She's on all fours underneath the picnic table; they both are, somehow. To her right, on the far side of Ana, is a sheer drop, the deck railing torn off, and Win falls onto her side and pulls Ana close. She vomits up water onto her back, apologizes, and Ana writhes around to face her and starts laughing, hard, through teeth that are grey with mud. She tucks her head against Win's chest and both of them lie still, for a while, growing aware of the sounds around them—shouts, the cries of children, car alarms, the sound of something falling and smashing below. Win puts her arms around Ana's head and looks up at the underside of the table, through the cracks between the slats, at the sky.

An hour later they're inside the cabin. It's sitting at an angle, now, but sloping away from the edge, so it seems safe enough. There are a handful of people here, busy people, unpacking the kits, bringing stuff outside, talking with Lena. A more permanent camp is being set up outside, islanders forming little groups, going back to their cars, checking the radio, booting up satellite phones. Win and Ana are lying down on a mildewed bed. They left the crowd in the main room without anyone noticing. By some miracle no one was badly hurt, at least not on top of the ridge—it's not clear what has happened to whoever was down there in the water's path. No one else has come up the road to Lena's old place. In her head, Win sees the boat go over and over, tumbling like a toy. The wave or whatever was left of it had knocked them off their feet, almost pulled the deck of the house off of its supports. Win didn't see anything else, just that massive concussion of water, but the people who were standing on the ridge had watched the wave run back into the ocean, had seen the wreckage revealed. It had scoured away everything on the northwestern tip of the island—the resort, the docks, the town centre. Lena's beach house and the others that clustered around the cove were gone, turned into toothpicks and scattered in the wake of the water. It had snipped the power lines and left the island black, had barricaded the highway with old-growth trees. The sun was going down over the smooth horizon. The cove was filled with debris, with shattered stems of telephone poles, signage, the bobbing shells of cars, orphaned bits of furniture. Everything on that side was gone, but the rest of the island was spared. The wave had ridden the shallow ravine that was left there for it by the passage of ancient glaciers, tearing up everything that fell in its circumscribed path. It was like it had decided what it was to do and then had done it, quickly and efficiently, laid waste with no wasted energy.

Looking out from the plateau, the island looked like a household pet come home from surgery, a patch of its wilderness shaved smooth into a triangle of stubble, brown with shattered trunks. Without trees there were no points of reference, only the washed-out ruins of the resort and, between it and the nude crescent of beach, a square of enclosed water held by a poured-concrete foundation. The sirens were quiet; the sky, now flat and placid, reflected grey in a new, long lake.

Lena comes into the bedroom and sits down on the bed. She's carrying two silver packets of dehydrated soup with little curlicues of steam coming out of them.

"It wasn't the 'Big One,' was it?" Win asks, sitting upright.

"No," Lena says, "of course not. If it was, we wouldn't be here."

"What about the other islands?"

"Skathis is as bad as this. The others are much less— just their shores, a little flooding. The mainland is fine."

"So what, it was just an earthquake?"

"Yes. A bad one, but just an earthquake."

"Nothing special?"

"Locally? Yes, it was. Special, that is. But geographically, no. At the tectonic scale this did not mean much. A minor disturbance."

"So there's more to come."

"There essentially always is."

NIGHT IS FALLING, AND FIRES ARE BEING LIT. THEY'RE still on the bed, Ana sleeping on top of the dusty covers. There's low conversation from the next room, things Win can't make out, but she can hear Marcus's voice, and Lena's. Her cast is on the floor, snipped open along one side by kitchen scissors, its plaster wet and loose, and her exposed foot is bone-white, shrivelled, like she's been in the bath for a month. She shoves back the pillow and lies flat.

Win is looking up at the ceiling, her waterlogged brain coming into and out of focus under its thin haze of sleep. It was all starting to feel like some kind of pattern, the punctuation of these awful events—these bodies falling, sinking underneath, over and over. The passenger, the surfer, the girl, then the island itself, and all of these points sprouting branches, folding back in on themselves, making new connections in her fuzzed-out head. Which of these came first? It's probably fatigue and shock and possibly even concussion, and it's probably just her own need to combine these things, these jolts and shudders, into something that coheres, but it could also be real. Something that is trying to tell her something.

Win tries to imagine what the island looks like from a satellite view—the long, dark stretch of it, a prehistoric, pre-industrial blackness, all of the light gathered up and compressed into an innermost glittering spine. What did this mean? People were making plans, taking inventory, figuring out the next steps. The homes on the ridge survived, as well as most of the leeward ones. The town centre, all of the stores, the greenmarket, the ferry terminal, were gone. Insurance, for those that had it, would be collected.

The Coast Guard would come; they would evacuate those who lived on the mainland, the tourists, the retirees. They'd comb the detritus, look for the bodies of the missing, if there were any missing. They'd gather everything into a pile, a zone of refuse. They'd put it on a barge and float it away. As soon as the boats got here, Win and Ana would leave, too; Lena would stay, would help regroup.

They'd take the van apart, salvage whatever could be salvaged, scrap the rest. The photographs, if there were any photographs, would be downloaded, scrubbed, reformatted. There would be news coverage, the circulation of smartphone videos, speeches by local politicians. Climate scientists would be interviewed, first responders, business owners. There would be a narrative. An apocalypse in preview, for the apocalypse-seekers. But what after that? When attention shifted elsewhere, when enough time had passed, and different kinds of interest started to accumulate? When the water had finally seeped back into the earth, when the roads were cleared, when the ferry service resumed, what then? What would come after all of this, and who would bring it about? Who would come to rebuild?

Win knows the answer to that question. It was them, of course; it was her and Ana and their boss and their clients. It was *them*, it always was. Who else?

THE END

DISCUSSION QUESTIONS

1. In what ways is the work being done by Win and Ana a continuation of the previous "reformatting" that has shaped and altered the small island? What common forces, or shared agendas, unite Win and Ana with the earlier history of Peliatos? How might they, as "agents" of this process, be distinct from their predecessors?

2. How does the setting of the novel impact its events? Might the same collisions and conspiracies have occurred elsewhere, or are these inextricably bound to an island that is both remote but also fairly accessible? Could *Last Tide* take place in an urban or suburban environment or, alternatively, somewhere even more remote than Peliatos?

3. Technology plays a key role in this novel, whether it be the heavily equipped "surveillance" van that Ana drives, the hardware and software behind Win's "face-blurring," the high-tech detection systems Lena uses to monitor tectonic activity, or Kitt's top-secret textiles. There is also, however, a pronounced presence of nature, and many of the novel's scenes treat this natural "background" as decidedly foregrounded. How might this story be seen as a working-through of the tensions between these two forces? Are there scenes in which technology and nature

collide in particularly loaded ways? Might the particular "tech" that features in this novel—360° cameras, hard drives, earthquake sensors, and hybrid fabrics—serve as metaphors or symbols for larger themes, and not just functional bits of gear?

4. Peliatos is fictional, but based on real-life locations in the Pacific Northwest—communities that, due to their closeness to affluent cities, have experienced a sudden influx of retirees and real estate investors, and now are in the midst of a massive, and often not welcome, demographic shift. This real estate boom is by no means a phenomenon specific to islands in the west coast of North America, and might indeed be happening in your own backyard. Do certain places come to mind? Have you experienced such processes of gentrification and development yourself, whether as a newcomer to a community or someone who's been displaced?

5. The setting of *Last Tide* is, in a sense, engineered to throw the struggle between these shifting demographics into sharper relief. What, then, are the particular aspects of Peliatos that seem to facilitate this "boom"? How about those that repel, or react against, this process? Has this been a push-and-pull playing out over the island's history? And, if so, what might be other moments in which the island's occupants have been displaced or even replaced outright? Finally, is it an "even battle," or is one side winning? How

does each character fit along this fault line—or is it more difficult than this to decipher who's on what side?

6. One of the key relationships of this novel is between Lena and her unexpected guests, Win and Ana. Their coming together is accidental, and is in fact caused by an accident, but once together they seem to form a functional trio. How does Lena's newfound role as caretaker fit with her larger role in the community of the island? How might Lena's own life experiences mirror that of her convalescent guests, and make her more immediately sympathetic to their situation?

7. What is the relationship between Win and Ana and the residents of the island? Do they feel a sense of distance, or one of community? Does this change over the course of the novel? Do the two of them feel equally at odds, or in harmony, with those who live on Peliatos? What role does Lena play in this, as a kind of "mediator"?

8. Different characters in the novel have a high sense of investment in these "big picture" events, whether as preppers, perpetrators, or professional scholars. Is there a difference between playing a willing, and an unwilling—or a knowing, and an unknowing—part in these events? To what extent might our knowledge of these ongoing crises be useful for us, or for our communities, even if we're not sure how to proceed to action? How might the extreme

case of the "Big One" serve as an illustration or counter-point to this value of knowledge? What is the point of trying to predict, or prepare for, these seemingly inevitable events, and what might be behind our desire to do so?

9. Win is surprised to learn that the majority of the island's residents are fully aware of the likelihood of the "Big One," and that many of them in fact moved to Peliatos after this knowledge was made widespread. Peliato's geographical location and exposed western edge makes it a likely candidate for total devastation in the event of the predicted earthquake; why, then, do people live there? Is it more of an obvious decision for some characters rather than others? How might this sense of ambient peril contribute to the feeling of community on the island?

10. The novel's four main characters each have their own section of narration, but the fifth key player in the novel—Marcus Farwell—does not. Why might this be the case? Would seeing inside of Marcus's head, and having his take on the events of the novel, be a problem for the narrative, in terms of suspense or of dramatic irony? What might you want to know from him, and how might his perspective be especially valuable? How do you imagine Marcus's sections would "read," in terms of voice and of events?

ACKNOWLEDGEMENTS

I am grateful to Matthew Tomkinson and Stephen Collis for reading early drafts of this novel; to Douglas Barbour, Claire Kelly, and Matt Bowes at NeWest Press, for their attentive support; to my parents, my brother, and to Daryn.

ANDY ZULIANI is a writer and multimedia artist who lives in the unceded territories of the Musqueam, Squamish, and Tsleil-Waututh Nations. He was born in the suburbs of Vancouver, and educated at Simon Fraser University and New York University. In his written and audio-visual work, he is drawn to the cultural afterlives of the 1960s; to the possibilities of ambience, tone, and collective feeling; and to narratives of crisis, of healing, and of improvised communities of care.